"What's wr
when I kisse

She averted her ~~~~~~ ~~ook her head. "You surprised me, that's all."

"And would you like me to kiss you now?"

She shook her head more emphatically and stood. "I think it would be best if you didn't. It would be wrong for me to get involved with you."

"And why is that?" Tris asked.

"Because you'll go home."

With that she turned and hurried to the door, leaving Tris to watch her retreat. The door slammed behind her with a startling finality.

If he'd thought he was making progress with Hallie, he'd been deluding himself. She'd run out of the house as if he'd posed a threat to her safety. What could have possibly put that idea into her head?

To my friend and fellow writer, Lori Handeland,
my resident expert on all things strange

And with special thanks to Mary Mayer Holmes,
who taught me everything I needed to know about clams.

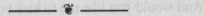

Kate Hoffmann is also the author of the following
novels in *Temptation*®:

INDECENT EXPOSURE
WANTED: WIFE
LOVE POTION # 9
LADY OF THE NIGHT
BACHELOR HUSBAND
THE STRONG SILENT TYPE
A HAPPILY UNMARRIED MAN
NEVER LOVE A COWBOY
THE PIRATE

WICKED WAYS

BY
KATE HOFFMANN

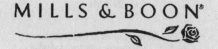

MILLS & BOON®

MILLS & BOON and MILLS & BOON with the Rose Device are registered trademarks of the publisher.
TEMPTATION is a registered trademark of Harlequin Enterprises Limited, used under licence.

First published in Great Britain 1997 by Harlequin Mills & Boon Limited, Eton House, 18-24 Paradise Road, Richmond, Surrey TW9 1SR

© Peggy Hoffmann 1996

ISBN 0 263 80220 5

21-9703

Printed and bound in Great Britain by BPC Paperbacks Limited, Aylesbury

1

THE WIND BLEW straight off the Atlantic in chilly gusts, rattling the nine-over-one windows of the Widow's Walk Inn and sending a whirlwind of autumn leaves down the dark cobblestone drive and into the silent streets of Egg Harbor, Maine. Rain drummed on the roof and waves crashed against the rocks at the base of the bluff, the roar audible through the old handmade glass panes.

Hallie Tyler looked up from her reservation book just in time to see a fleeting shadow pass by the window that overlooked the wraparound porch. She waited for the front door of the inn to open, for the tiny bell above the door to jingle. But when it didn't after a few moments, she rubbed her tired eyes and shook her head. After such a hectic day, it was no wonder she was imagining another guest arrival. It was nearly midnight and all her guests should be sound asleep upstairs. No one would be out and about on a night such as this.

Her gaze fell on the folded copy of the *New York Times*'s Travel and Leisure section. She picked it up and skimmed the brief article that had caused such an unusual onslaught of business so late in the season.

Egg Harbor, Maine, September 23—The Widow's Walk Inn, run by proprietress Hallie Tyler, was built as the summer retreat of nineteenth-

*century Boston shipping tycoon Lucas Tyler. Lo-
cated on the rugged coast of Maine in the picturesque town of Egg Harbor, the twelve-room inn
was once home to the legendary Nicholas Tyler,
who was said to be a vampire. Buried in the family plot after a drowning accident, Nicholas is ru-
mored to rise from the grave on the night of each
new moon to wander the streets of Egg Harbor in
search of innocent victims.*

"What a crock," she muttered, tossing the paper
aside.

The last thing she needed now was the resurrection
of that moldy old vampire legend. The outlandish tale
had dogged her family for as long as she could remember. If it had been up to Hallie, Nicholas Tyler and his
bloodthirsty bent would have stayed buried in the little vine-twisted graveyard that sat between her property and the rest of the town. But her elderly maiden
aunts, Patience and Prudence, had solicited the *Times*
review and had delightedly told the reporter about old
Uncle Nick's strange drinking habits and his oversize
eyeteeth.

Hallie shook her head and smiled wearily. The aunts
had only been trying to help, taking seriously her sug-
gestion that they turn their energies toward the proper
marketing of the inn and away from their sudden interest in UFOs and alien life forms. She'd just never expected their bumbling attempts to have a positive effect
on her business.

The aunts—her great-aunts, actually—had been
Hallie's responsibility since her parents had passed
away over ten years before. Samuel and Clarissa Tyler

had left Hallie, their only child, the deed to the old family house, a huge Queen Anne-style monstrosity that sat on a bluff above the Atlantic.

Most of the townsfolk expected her to sell and remain in Boston at her advertising job. But she'd been raised at Tyler House, and had spent an idyllic childhood in Egg Harbor with her parents and aunts. When the money ran out and the taxes were two years overdue, she'd had no choice but to come back and save the home she loved so much.

It hadn't taken her more than a moment to decide. She quit her job, abandoned her life in the city along with the man she planned to marry, and returned to a place that had always been safe and secure—the only place she'd ever truly been happy.

Without a regular job and with the aunts to support, she'd been forced by finances to turn the house into an inn. A small but loyal clientele kept the books just barely in the black, which was enough for Hallie. She'd never wanted to run a tourist trap like so many of the inns along the coast of Maine, from Kennebunkport to Bar Harbor. But Patience and Prudence, full of octogenarian energy, wanted Hallie's inn to be a rousing success and they wouldn't stop until it was so.

The aunts had been beside themselves with excitement when the review had appeared a week ago. And from that moment on Hallie's life had been an endless whirl of inn-keeping duties, of demanding guests and unmade beds, of early breakfasts and late-night bookkeeping. And unending questions about Uncle Nick.

The rush didn't promise to let up until the winter set in. The Widow's Walk Inn was completely booked for the next month with guests more interested in the Tyler family vampire than in strolling the picturesque town of Egg Harbor.

Vampires, she thought to herself. Only a fool would believe in the existence of the undead. Hallie was much too practical to consider Dracula and his black-caped buddies any more than just fiction. Her uncle was no more a vampire than she was the creature from the Black Lagoon.

A cold draft of damp salt air suddenly wafted around her, causing the pages of the reservation book to flutter. She shivered and rubbed her arms, then glanced up to find a man standing in the shadows of the open door, silently watching her.

Startled, Hallie sucked in a sharp breath and placed her fingers over her lips to keep from crying out. She hadn't heard the creaky hinge that she'd been meaning to oil for weeks, nor the jingle that usually announced an arrival. And she'd just locked the front door a few hours before, hadn't she?

"May I come in?" he asked softly, his words drifting toward her on the cold night air.

"Of . . . of course," Hallie replied, hardly able to find her voice. "Can I help you?"

The man closed the door, then stepped out of the shadows into the soft pink glow from the old electrified oil lamp sitting on the end of the front desk. He was dressed entirely in black—turtleneck, Levi's jeans and a flowing trench coat with the collar pulled up around his neck. His hair, straight and windblown, was as dark as his clothing and nearly reached his shoulders. He tipped his chin up and light played along the hawklike planes and angles of his face, revealing the rough stubble of his beard. A pair of eyes, the palest blue, met her gaze and she shivered again, startled by the unearthly color.

"I'd like a room," he said. "Something quiet."

Hallie stared at him, transfixed by a gaze that acted on her senses like a mind-numbing drug and a voice that seemed almost hypnotic. "Something quiet," she murmured, letting the memory of his voice warm her blood like fine brandy on a cold winter's night.

"Do you have a room, then?" he asked.

Hallie blinked, startled for a moment by the strange haze that clouded her thoughts. "I—I'm sorry," she replied. "We're full for this evening."

He seemed surprised by her statement and raised a dark eyebrow. "But I was assured that no reservation was necessary midweek," he replied smoothly. "It is late September, well past the peak tourist season."

Hallie smiled apologetically, still unable to draw her eyes away from his striking features. "Normally we would have a room, but the inn was featured in last weekend's *New York Times*."

His jaw tensed in irritation and he cursed softly. "Are you sure? You must have at least one room left, just for the night."

"Every room is full," Hallie said. "I'm sorry. This is quite unusual. We never have a full house, since we're pretty far north and a good distance . . ." She suddenly realized she was babbling, telling him things he already knew. "Off the main highway," she finished lamely.

"Maybe you could recommend another place to stay? It must be peaceful. I need . . . solitude."

"There is no place else here in town. We're the only inn or hotel within twenty-five miles. You'll have to drive back up the peninsula and head back south."

He ran impatient fingers through his long raven-black hair and shook his head. "I've been driving for nearly eight hours. It's midnight. There has to be someplace closer I can stay."

Hallie hesitated. She had already turned six guests away that night for lack of reservations. Why was she suddenly concerned about the comfort of this particular man? It wasn't her fault he'd driven halfway to nowhere without the benefit of a reservation. Hadn't he thought to pick up a phone?

"Well?" he prompted.

"Well, there is our coach house," she said. "I've begun to renovate it into a guest cottage, but the central heating system is a little balky. If you keep the fireplaces going, you'll be fine for the night. It's on a deserted corner of the property and it's very quiet. You'll have to come to the inn for breakfast."

"I don't eat breakfast," he said. "And if the room is acceptable, I'd like to stay for two weeks." He pulled a wad of bills from his pocket and pushed it at her without bothering to count the money.

She looked down at the crumpled bills. "But the coach house is in the midst of renovation. It's all right for one night, but not really fit for—"

"I'd prefer to judge that for myself," he said. "And I will pay extra to have dinner brought to me," he said, almost as an afterthought.

"We usually don't offer lunch or dinner to our guests," Hallie began, meeting his mesmerizing gaze again. "But . . . but I suppose I could do that."

"Good," he said, his intense expression softening a bit.

She counted his money, surprised to find nearly two thousand dollars in her hands. "This is more than enough." She handed half back to him.

"It's only money," he said, a hint of contempt in his voice. He pushed it back at her. "Keep the extra. I have no better use for it. It can't buy me what I need right now."

Startled by his sudden change in mood, Hallie grabbed a registration card and a pen. "Your name?" she asked.

"My name?" He paused for a moment. "Tristan...Edward Tristan."

She wrote his name in her register, then handed him a card. "Just fill in your address, Mr. Tristan."

A few moments later, his registration complete, she plucked a pair of keys off the board. "I'll get my coat and a flashlight and show you the way," she said.

He was standing on the porch, the salt-saturated wind whipping through his hair and the rain spattering his face, when she returned from her small suite at the back of the house. Hallie pulled the hood of her slicker over her head and started down the steps in her knee-high wellies. "We'll have to walk," she said. "It's a bit of a trek in this nasty weather and the path is muddy. Do you have luggage?"

He pointed to a garment bag, a leather duffel and a small shoulder tote, all black, near the rail of the porch. With easy movements, he swung the luggage over his shoulder and joined her at the bottom of the steps.

Hallie bent her head against the wind and set off across the yard for the northwest corner of the property, anxious to get her last guest settled so she could get to bed herself. He matched every two of her strides with one of his and set a pace faster than her own. As she walked beside him, she realized how tall he was, at least an inch or two over six feet, with broad shoulders that seemed even broader in the trench coat.

Halfway to the coach house, she slipped in the slick mud and he reached out to steady her. His hand remained firmly on her elbow for the balance of their walk, the gesture faintly protective, even possessive. She gave him a sideways glance, but found his eyes focused on the path ahead.

Out of the blackness and the mist, the coach house appeared, a rough stone building with a slate roof. The small house had once guarded the entrance to the property, but over the past century the town had abandoned the North Road, replacing it with a road that ran closer to the southern edge of Hallie's property and the inn. Now, all that was left was a rusted iron gate covered with brush and vines.

She'd always loved the little house. When she was a child, it had served as a wonderful fantasy castle. And someday, after she'd paid off all her bills and loans, she planned to move from her small suite of rooms in the inn and live in the coach house. But for now, it was just another room to rent, a room to be occupied by the enigmatic Mr. Tristan.

She stopped at the front door and looked up at him. "I—I'll just show you inside," she said. She unlocked the door, then held out the keys to him. Slowly, he covered her hand with his, his fingers warm and firm on hers. She shivered, not from the cold and damp, but from the unbidden current of attraction she felt for him.

Hastily, Hallie snatched her fingers away. "The second key is for the front door of the inn. We lock the door after midnight but you may want to get in after hours."

She opened the coach house door and flipped on the lights. The far wall of the great room was cluttered with construction supplies—lumber, drywall, tools. Hallie watched as he took in his surroundings, certain that he'd be spending just one night, yet strangely disappointed at the prospect. He wandered back into the bedroom with its adjoining bath, then appeared at the doorway. He gave only a cursory glance at the tiny kitchen.

"Did your contractor quit?" he asked.

"I've been doing most of the work myself," she replied, rubbing her hands together, more to still the tingling than to warm them. "I blew the budget on the bathroom. I can't go much further until I take care of the heating problems. I'll start a fire for you in the bedroom to take the dampness out of the air."

Their gazes met again and held. Droplets of rain sparkled on his dark lashes and the light gleamed off his damp cheekbones. He shook his head. "There's no need. Just tell me where the firewood is and I'll take care of it."

"It's out here, around the corner of the house, beneath a tarp. Matches are on the mantel, kindling in the basket. The phone is next to the sofa. Just call if you need something."

Suddenly uneasy, he turned and walked to the window, then stared out into the black night. "Then I suppose I have everything I need for now, Miss . . ."

"Hallie," she said. "Hallie Tyler."

"Hallie," he repeated. "It's an unusual name."

"It's really Halimeda. An old family name."

He slowly faced her. "It's Greek," he said with a half smile.

"What?"

"Your name. It's Greek. It means 'dreaming of the sea.'" He looked directly into her eyes. "Do you?"

"Do I?"

"Do you dream?" he asked.

She frowned, unable to tell if he was serious or simply teasing her. She barely knew him, but Edward Tristan didn't seem the type to tease. She smiled hesitantly. "I—I guess I do," she murmured. "Doesn't everyone?"

"Not everyone," he replied. He took a deep breath, then turned back to the window. "That will be all, Miss Tyler. I'm sure I'll get along just fine here."

His tone was dismissive and Hallie bristled slightly. "Well, if you need anything," she said, "just call."

He didn't hear her, or if he did, he chose not to respond. He continued to stare, unblinking, out the moisture-streaked glass into the darkness. Hallie quietly let herself out and started back toward the inn. As she walked through the rain, her mind dwelled on her newest guest.

She had met many people in her years as an innkeeper, but never had she encountered a man like Edward Tristan. Outwardly, he seemed normal enough. In fact, he was most likely one of the most handsome men she'd ever laid eyes on. And that body, tall and lithe and athletic, broad shoulders and a narrow waist, and long, muscular legs.

But for a man with such obvious physical attributes, he seemed uncomfortable in her presence. On first sight, she would have assumed him to be the ultimate charmer, a man with a quick smile and a glib line. Instead, he was aloof, distracted, nearly to the point of rudeness, holding himself above the pleasantries of idle conversation and good manners.

In any other man, she would have sensed pure conceit. But Edward Tristan was more than just the sum of his outward attributes. The man seemed troubled, as if he'd come to the Widow's Walk Inn to escape rather than relax.

A proper innkeeper would try to draw him out, to loosen that tightly coiled spring inside him and encourage him to find some respite here on the coast of Maine. But she suspected that Mr. Tristan would not welcome her efforts. The man wanted to be alone and she wasn't about to try to change his mind.

Besides, after her rather startling reaction to his touch, she'd be better off to stay as far away from him as possible. After all, a proper innkeeper did *not* lust after her guests.

TRIS STARED out the window and watched as Hallie Tyler disappeared into the darkness. He would have liked for her to stay; he knew he'd be awake—and alone—until dawn. He'd been so long without the company of a woman that he could listen for hours to Hallie's musical voice, drink in her delicate features and inhale her sweet perfume.

He led such a solitary life that he'd begun to wonder whether he'd lost all capacity to interact with people. How did one approach a woman like Hallie Tyler? What was there to talk about? She was nothing like the other women he'd had in his life, women who had so much to say about themselves that he rarely needed to speak. Women well aware of who and what he was—and always eager to please.

Edward Tristan, guest at the Widow's Walk Inn, was known to the rest of the world as Tristan Montgomery. That name was now as familiar to readers as King and Koontz, masters of the horror genre. After Tris's last three hardcovers hit the *New York Times*'s list, he had joined the rarefied circle of authors who could guarantee an instant bestseller by simply putting his name on a book cover.

But the pressure to produce another number-one book had become unbearable. For the past six months, hounded by his agent and his editor, Tris had been in the grip of a major writer's block, unable to write more than a few poorly plotted paragraphs a day. He had burned out, feeling as if every drop of creativity had been drained from his body.

When his agent suggested a change of scenery, Tris had relented, ready to try anything to break his literary gridlock. His agent had assured him the Widow's Walk Inn was the perfect place to relax and work on his new book. Unfortunately, Louise had missed the article in last weekend's *Times* that had turned the inn into Maine's newest hot spot.

But the coach house would do for now. At least he wouldn't have to put up with the cult of fans that hung out in front of his Upper East Side apartment. Or the stress of day-to-day living in Manhattan. Or the many and frequent distractions available in the city.

Here, with nothing else to do, he'd be forced to work. The only distraction would be an occasional look at

Hallie Tyler's pretty face when she brought him his dinner.

A soft ring startled him from his silent revery. Tris reached into his pocket and pulled out his cellular phone, then flipped it open.

"So, are you writing yet?"

Tris recognized his agent's voice on the other end of the line. "I was sleeping, Louise."

"Don't lie to me, darling," she said. "I know your work habits and you're strictly nocturnal. You never go to bed before 5:00 a.m. Now, tell me, how's it going?"

"It isn't," Tris said. "I just got here. I registered under Edward Tristan. Hopefully, that will keep the press and the fans at bay."

"You are such a clever boy. Does it look like the place will be conducive to writing?"

"I don't know yet, Louise," Tris replied. "If you'd hang up, I could get out my computer and see."

"Darling, you know I don't want to pressure you, but if you don't have a first draft in by Christmas, we're in serious trouble. You won't get your summer release date."

"I'll finish," Tris said.

"Well, just to make certain, I'll send you something for inspiration."

"No more gifts," Tris said. "That damn raven you sent me last year has eaten me out of house and home."

"How is dear little Edgar Allan Crow?"

"He's a hell of a lot bigger and he's staying with friends. If he gives them any trouble, I've told them to call you. And if you continue to harass me, I'll make sure you have a raven for a houseguest next time I leave town." He paused. "I thought you told me this place would be peaceful. I almost didn't get a room. The place was full, so the innkeeper had to put me up in an old coach house. Some business with an article in the *New York Times.*"

"Really? I didn't read that. But why worry over it now? You do have a room, don't you?"

"But the town is crawling with tourists. I won't even be able to go out."

"That's probably for the best, darling. By the way, how much *do* you have done?"

"Quite a bit, actually," Tris lied. He hadn't written a single page since he'd pitched the book six months ago. But he wasn't about to tell Louise the truth. If she knew, she'd be calling him ten times a day instead of just five.

"How much?" she prodded.

"Louise, I'm going to hang up. Then I'm going to walk to the bluff and throw this phone into the Atlantic. The next time you get an answer at this number, you'll be bugging someone in Iceland."

Tris snapped the phone shut and slipped it into his coat pocket, then grabbed his room key and headed for the door. As he passed his luggage, he glanced down at the case that held his laptop computer. He felt only a small twinge of guilt before he opened the door and walked outside. He would have plenty of time to write. Right now, he needed to think.

The rain had stopped and a half moon hung low in the east. Black clouds scudded across the sky on the brisk wind and the tang of salt touched his nose as soon as he stepped out the door. He waited for a moment until his eyes adjusted to the dark, then set off toward the sound of the ocean.

From the top of the rocky bluff he could see the small harbor below. Lights at the head of each pier illuminated a small fleet of fishing trawlers. The boats bobbed at their moorings, awaiting sunrise and the arrival of their crews. Below him, at the edge of the water, large boulders lined the narrow beach, the surf surging between them.

He turned back to stare at the inn, set on top of a small rise. The house was a sprawling piece of architecture constructed of white clapboard and fish-scale shingles. The bay windows sported multipaned sashes, and spindles and brackets decorated the long porch and the gable peaks. A narrow walk surrounded the third-story turret, giving the inn its name.

Tris raked his hands through his hair and closed his eyes. His thoughts drifted back to Hallie Tyler, to her fresh-faced beauty and her hesitant smile. She hadn't seemed to recognize him and he wondered whether she'd ever read one of his books. People were always surprised upon meeting him. He imagined they expected some strange fiend with a slightly warped mind and maniacal eyes.

It felt good to put those expectations aside, to wander through his days and nights like he used to, unnoticed, unknown. He'd never wanted fame. He only wanted to make a living at writing. Now he made more money than he could possibly need, yet he couldn't walk down the streets of New York without being recognized. He had tried to cut back on the media appearances, hoping that might help, but his fans—and his publicist—were persistent.

Could he hope to remain incognito in Egg Harbor? Or would it only be a matter of time before his alter ego,

Tristan Montgomery, was recognized? This little sea-coast town was far from a hotbed of media activity, so maybe he'd be safe. Maybe, for just a little while longer, he'd be able to be himself.

"I'll give it a week, tops," Tris murmured.

He stepped closer to the edge of the bluff, then reached into his pocket and grabbed his cell phone. In one smooth motion, he lofted the phone into the air and watched as, glinting in the moonlight, it landed in the roiling surf. Satisfied, he started back toward the house, then decided to make a more detailed exploration.

An hour later, just as the moon reached its highest point in the sky, he happened upon an old cemetery. An iron fence choked with vines surrounded the grave-yard. The gate screeched in protest as he stepped in-side. He stood and listened to the wind whistling in the trees above him, surveying the crooked rows of weath-ered stone grave markers, the tall obelisks and pale headstones gleaming white in the moonlight.

He smiled to himself. He loved graveyards. In fact, he loved almost anything that caused a prickle to rise on the back of his neck and a shiver to skitter along his spine. He'd become a student of fear and the effect it had on the human mind and body. Fear and terror had be-come the tools of his trade and there was nothing he liked better than to feel the rush of adrenaline that ac-companied a good scare.

If ever he needed inspiration, it was now. He stared into the night and imagined zombies and ghoulies and other horrific monsters appearing out of the dark. Lowering himself to the damp ground, he closed his eyes and drew a deep breath, the scent of decomposing leaves and wet grass teasing at his senses.

Tris wasn't sure how long he sat on the edge of the graveyard, letting his mind wander and his skin prickle. Spurred by the eerie atmosphere of the graveyard, he carefully constructed the main character of his novel, piece by piece, feature by feature.

He'd begun with a man, but his thoughts kept returning to a woman—a woman with perfect features and silky dark hair, brilliant green eyes and a cupid's bow mouth. A woman just like Hallie Tyler. He'd never written a book from a heroine's point of view, but suddenly it seemed like the perfect solution. His mind raced with all the possibilities as he carefully brought the character to life in his head.

The moon had long ago set by the time he had his heroine all worked out. He sensed that the sun would be up in another hour and suddenly he felt the tug of exhaustion—both mental and physical. He levered himself to his feet, then brushed his hands on his thighs.

He was chilled to the bone but he felt good—alive and aware—as if all the clutter in his mind had been swept away and the seeds of his story had appeared in astounding clarity.

It wasn't the story he'd promised to write. It was better. Both his editor and agent would have no trouble seeing that. Tris started back to the inn, whistling a soft tune. This place would be good for him. Here he'd be able to work again.

A RAUCOUS BUZZ penetrated Hallie's dreams, drawing her out of a fitful sleep. With a moan, she slapped at the alarm clock, finally silencing the intrusive sound when the clock tumbled onto the plush Oriental carpet.

"Serves you right," she mumbled, pulling the pillow over her head.

She felt as if she hadn't slept at all. Her rest had been troubled, frustrated and tormented by strange images and hazy dreams. Several times when she'd wakened, she could have sworn there was someone in the room with her. Holding her breath, she had listened for any sound, but all she'd heard was the wind outside, the soft hiss of rain against the old panes of glass and the gentle whisper of the lace curtains as they'd fluttered against the drafty window.

It was as if someone had invaded her sleep and slipped silently into her dreams. Pinching her eyes shut, Hallie tried to put a face to the vague images that had haunted her thoughts. Midnight-black hair...aquiline nose, a firm, sensual mouth . . . and pale blue eyes.

Hallie groaned and threw her arm over her face. She'd been dreaming about Edward Tristan. Strange, disturbing dreams filled with hazy longing and bewildering desire. Good grief, the man was a complete stranger. What had gotten into her?

Sitting up in her bed, Hallie rubbed her eyes. She was simply overtired. She'd dreamed about the man because he was the last person she'd talked to before she'd fallen asleep. There was nothing more to it. It wasn't as if she harbored some secret sexual fantasy about him.

Sure he was handsome. To be truthful, he was downright sexy. But she had to admit, he was also just a little bit odd. All that black and those strange, unearthly eyes, and his unsettling detachment. He reminded her of a caged panther, restless and dangerous, always watching with a perceptive and predatory gaze.

Hallie tumbled out of bed, determined to put Mr. Tristan out of her mind. She clumsily pulled on a T-shirt and a pair of sweatpants, then padded to the bathroom in her bare feet to brush her teeth and comb her hair.

A few minutes later, after turning on the lights and unlocking the front door, Hallie headed for the kitchen, ready to begin her day. It was 5:00 a.m., at least an hour away from sunrise. Breakfast was served between seven and nine. She usually took care of the work in the kitchen, with Prudence and Patience handling the service to guests and the cleanup.

She put the coffee on first, then opened the huge stainless-steel refrigerator and pulled out a bag of wild blueberries that she'd defrosted the night before. As she began to assemble the ingredients for her famous Widow's Walk muffins, she had the sudden eerie feeling that she wasn't alone.

"Is it too early for breakfast?"

Hallie spun around to find Edward Tristan standing in the doorway of the kitchen, his arms crossed over his chest, his shoulder braced on the doorjamb. "Mr. Tristan!" she cried. Her heart leapt into her throat and she blinked in shock. Good grief, the man had an uncanny knack for sneaking up on her. He could enter a room without a sound!

"Tris," he said, gazing distractedly around the kitchen. "You should call me Tris. Everyone does."

"What are you doing up at this hour?"

"I haven't gone to bed yet," he replied in a matter-of-fact tone. "I'm kind of a night person."

She frowned. "Where were you?" she asked. "You're all muddy."

He glanced down at his clothes, then stared at his hands, turning them over in front of his face as if his disheveled appearance surprised even him. "The graveyard," he said.

"You were at the graveyard?"

"Yes. It's a very nice graveyard as graveyards go." He slid onto a stool at the end of the trestle table and watched her openly.

"Have you visited many?" Hallie asked.

A smile quirked the corners of his mouth. "A fair number. It's very old, your graveyard."

"It's not mine, it belongs to the Episcopal Church in Egg Harbor. And, yes, it is old."

"Mmm," he replied, his attention caught by the egg-beater. He slowly turned the handle and watched the beaters spin 'round and 'round. "Would you have any coffee made?"

"Regular or decaf?"

"Decaf," he replied. "Regular will keep me up all day long."

Hallie raised her brows, then decided not to question his bizarre sleeping habits. She grabbed a mug from the tall, glass-fronted cabinets, poured him a cup and placed it in front of him. He held the coffee mug in both hands, breathed in the steam, then set it down without taking a sip. "It's chilly outside," he murmured.

She gave him a shrewd glance. "So, I guess you're one of those vampire watchers, huh?"

His gaze snapped back to hers and he stared at her, a frown wrinkling his forehead. "Vampire watchers?"

"You've come to Egg Harbor to search for my uncle Nicholas, the Tyler family vampire, haven't you?"

"And I thought *I* had a strange family," he said. He chuckled, an intoxicating sound that washed over Hallie in waves. "A vampire? This is very...interesting. Tell me more."

"I don't believe the story," Hallie said defensively, waving a wooden spoon in his direction. "There are no such things as vampires."

"What makes you so certain?" he challenged. "This world is filled with strange and fantastic creatures. Why not vampires?"

"I can't believe you didn't know about Nicholas," she said. "That's why the inn is booked, you know. Everyone's come to Egg Harbor, hoping to run into a real live vampire."

"Dead," Tris said.

"What?"

"A real *dead* vampire," he corrected.

Hallie smiled. "Whatever. It's just that Egg Harbor has always been a nice, peaceful little town. I'd rather it weren't suddenly overrun with tourists. Especially the type who are only here to see a real *dead* vampire."

Tris slowly twisted his coffee mug between his palms. "But wouldn't more tourists be good for your business?"

"I have enough to live on now. I don't need more, especially at the expense of this town. This is one of the only places on the coast that hasn't been spoiled and I've worked very hard to keep it that way. Egg Harbor is almost unchanged from the way it was when I was a child."

"You've lived in this house your entire life?" Tris asked.

Hallie nodded. "Except for college and six years in Boston. The house has been in my family since the late nineteenth century. My great-great grandfather built it in 1883 as his summer residence. He was a shipping tycoon in Boston."

"This is a long ride from Boston," Tris said.

"He and his family used to sail here every summer on one of his clipper ships. They dropped anchor in the harbor and rowed ashore."

"So was he the vampire?"

Hallie grabbed the eggbeater laying in front of him and began to mix the ingredients for her muffins. "Actually the vampire was Lucas's son, Nicholas. My great-great-uncle. He died in 1923. My great-aunts, Prudence and Patience, know more about him than I do. They both live here at the inn. They're responsible for the *New York Times*'s review." She glanced up. "You don't really believe in vampires, do you?"

Tris shrugged and slipped off his stool. "The jury's still out on that one. But I wouldn't write off the possibility."

Hallie stared at him and shook her head in disbelief. She spread the muffin tins out in front of her and began to fill the cups with batter.

"I always try to keep an open mind." He wandered over to the refrigerator. "Could I get something to eat?"

Hallie nodded. "Don't open that tuna salad," she warned. "I'm waiting for it to walk out on its own. There's leftover meatloaf and rolls for a sandwich."

He stood at the refrigerator, staring into it for a long time as if waiting for something appealing to call out to him. Hallie put the muffin tins in the double oven, then plopped down on a stool and sipped her coffee.

She braced her chin in her palm and yawned, watching him as he picked through the contents of her refrigerator. Slowly her eyes fluttered shut and she allowed her thoughts to drift for a moment.

She wasn't sure when she dozed off, or how long she slept. But when she opened her eyes she could see the sun peeking above the horizon, its first rays shining through the window over the sink. The aroma of baked blueberry muffins filled the kitchen and she drew a deep breath. She closed her eyes and nestled her head into the crook of her arm that rested on the trestle table.

Her eyes popped open. "Damn!" Hallie bolted upright, stumbled off the stool and raced to the oven. But when she pulled the door open, she found the oven empty. "Where are my muffins?" She shook her head, certain that she'd put the muffins in the oven.

Hallie spun around, then noticed the six muffin pans lined up on the tile countertop. Frowning, she looked back inside the oven, then over at the counter. Realization slowly dawned and she smiled.

"Tris," she murmured. She let the sound of his name drift off her lips on a whisper. An image of him flashed in her mind and she closed her eyes and enjoyed it for a brief moment.

"Asleep on your feet?" Hallie's aunt Prudence stood in the doorway to the dining room, a tiny figure dressed in a pretty flowered dress, her white hair tucked into a knot at her nape, pearl earrings and a necklace completing her ensemble. Prudence and Patience were nearly eighty years old, but the aunts sometimes looked as fresh-faced as teenagers.

"Just resting my eyes," Hallie said. "I didn't sleep much last night. Where's Patience?"

"She's flirting with that Mr. Markham, our overly bold egg man." Prudence shook her head and clucked her tongue. "You know he's been married *three* times. And he is a younger man."

Hallie gave her aunt a sideways glance. "He's seventy-six."

"And that's too young for a woman of her advanced years. Sister positively melts when the man appears, batting her eyelashes and throwing herself at him like some…painted hussy. Our poor departed mother must be turning over in her grave at such brazen behavior."

Hallie giggled. Her aunts had never married, though she suspected there had been many suitors along the way. But Patience and Prudence were devoted to each other and their many social causes. Raised in the Puritan atmosphere of small-town New England, they had become the social conscience of Egg Harbor.

"We have a full house," Hallie said. "You and Patience better be ready for a rush at breakfast."

Prudence poured herself a cup of coffee. "This is so exciting. I saw Mayor Pemberton downtown yesterday and gave him a copy of the *Times*'s review. He plans to discuss our sudden tourism boom at the village board meeting Thursday night. He's always been high on tourism."

"Prudence!" Hallie cried. "I told you that I didn't want you pushing this vampire stuff. It's not true. And I don't want you talking to Silas Pemberton."

"How do you know it's not true?"

Hallie sighed. "I suppose I'm going to have to go down to the meeting and put an end to all this silliness."

Prudence reached over and patted Hallie's hand. "Whatever you want, dear. But I think all this vampire business could be good for *our* business." With that, Prudence grabbed her coffee mug and bustled out of the kitchen.

Hallie stared after her and shook her head wearily. There were definitely days when running a lovely inn on the idyllic coast of Maine was not all it was cracked up to be.

2

PATIENCE HELD the tray out in front of her. "He hasn't touched his dinner," she said, her voice breathy with astonishment.

"They don't eat, you know," Prudence replied knowingly from her spot at the kitchen sink.

"No need, I suppose," Patience added in the odd way that the aunts had of finishing each other's thoughts. There were times that Hallie would swear they shared the same brain. Each one knew what the other was thinking at any given moment. After almost eighty years of life as twins, Patience and Prudence had developed a disconcerting telepathic communication that not even Hallie was privy to.

Hallie looked up from her pastry-making and frowned at them both. "What do you mean, *they* don't eat? Who?"

"Vampires, dear," Prudence said.

"The undead," Patience added.

Hallie put her rolling pin down on the marble slab and hitched her fists on her hips. "Haven't I warned you not to bring up that vampire business again? We're the laughingstock of Egg Harbor. And we've got an innful of loony tunes, all here hoping to run into a real vampire. I want things here to return to normal and they won't if you keep chattering on about vampires."

"I didn't bring it up, dear," Patience exclaimed. "Sister did. She believes that Mr. Tristan is one of...*them*."

"A vampire hunter?"

"No," she whispered. "A real vampire. Come to visit our dear uncle Nicholas."

"On the night of the new moon," Patience added.

Hallie groaned in frustration and pressed the heels of her hands to her temples. "You two have got to stop with this. You can't continue to perpetuate this silly legend. We all know it's not true. And now you're making up stories about one of our guests."

"Mr. Tristan," Prudence said.

"He didn't eat his dinner," Patience said. "And he said we needn't bring him dinner unless he specifically calls for it."

"And that means he's a vampire?" Hallie asked. "Maybe Mr. Tristan wasn't hungry. Maybe he doesn't like shepherd's pie or sourdough bread."

"Maybe he prefers fresh blood for his dinner," Patience added enthusiastically.

"That is not what I meant!" Hallie cried. "Just because he wasn't hungry doesn't mean the man is a vampire."

Prudence wagged her finger. "Oh, but there are other clues, dear. He's been with us for three full days and not once have we seen him during the daylight hours."

Patience nodded in agreement. "And he is a bit pale," she added.

"And his eyes," Prudence said. "The last time I looked into them they were positively red."

"Sister and I have decided to keep an eye on him," Patience said. "Heaven knows, having a real vampire staying at Widow's Walk would be a boon to business.

Do you think he might agree to an appearance for our
guests?"

"You will leave Mr. Tristan alone," Hallie snapped.
"I won't have you disturbing him, especially with your
silly vampire fantasies. He simply wants some peace
and quiet, that's all!"

Hallie bit her bottom lip and slowly counted to ten.
She shouldn't get so impatient with the Sisters; they really meant no harm. And over the years she'd come to
truly enjoy their company.

After her parents died, she had felt an overwhelming emptiness, as if she'd been deserted, left alone to
fend for herself. The Sisters had slowly drawn her out,
making her see that she still had a family—they were
her family now. But every now and then she still felt the
loneliness, a sense of isolation pressing down on her.

"Vampires like it quiet," Patience ventured.

"That's true, Sister," Prudence said.

Startled out of her thoughts, Hallie glanced at her
aunts. They hadn't paid an ounce of attention to her
pleas. Once they'd made up their collective mind, there
wasn't much Hallie could do. And they seemed fixated
on this vampire legend. She sighed. "If I can get Mr.
Tristan to eat his dinner, will you promise to leave him
alone?" she asked.

The pair looked at each other, then turned to Hallie
and nodded their assent. "You would have to see him
eat," Prudence said.

"Or it would prove nothing," Patience added.

Hallie snatched the tray out of her aunt's hands and
tossed the cold shepherd's pie into the garbage. "I'll
prove to you both that the only vampire at the Wid-

ow's Walk is haunting those overactive imaginations of yours."

Determined to prove her aunts' theories false, Hallie hurriedly put together another dinner tray, choosing the tastiest morsels from her kitchen—a hearty onion soup, a smoked chicken salad sandwich with imported cheese, and a huge slice of sour apple pie with home-made vanilla ice cream.

Hallie had managed to avoid Mr. Tristan over the past few days. But now, she'd be forced to come face-to-face with the man who had plagued her thoughts since the night of his arrival. The past three nights she'd faced a sleep filled with the same strange, unsettling images, always waking with the distinct impression that a presence had invaded her dreams and that someone had stood over her bed just a moment before she woke.

She rationalized the dreams as a result of her self-imposed celibacy. She hadn't had a date in years and could count the number of men she'd gone out with on one hand. In Egg Harbor, single men of her generation were single for one reason only—no woman in her right mind would choose to marry them.

But Edward Tristan wasn't from Egg Harbor. Edward Tristan was an attractive and mysterious stranger from New York City, a man any sex-starved woman might find herself fantasizing about. Not that Hallie was sex-starved. She was simply feeling a few hunger pangs, especially when she looked into those incredible blue eyes of his and gazed upon that lean, muscular body.

"Don't forget this!" Prudence said. She retrieved a garlic bulb from a long rope that hung near the refrigerator. Carefully, she placed it on the tray. "Just in case," she murmured. "Vampires hate garlic."

Hallie pushed the garlic off the tray, then balanced it on her hip and opened the back door, grabbing the flashlight from a shelf beside the door. "You'll see," she said as Prudence and Patience watched her speculatively. "Mr. Tristan will eat every last crumb!"

Hallie hurried down the dark path to the coach house. As she approached, she noticed only one light shining through the great room window into the dark night. She rapped sharply on the door, then repeated her summons twice more before he answered.

"Yes, what is it?" he muttered in an irritated tone. He didn't bother to look up, merely opened the door and continued to stare at a piece of paper he held in his hand.

"I—I've brought you dinner," Hallie said, holding out the tray.

His gaze snapped up to meet hers and he blinked hard, as if she had interrupted some deep contemplation. He glanced down at the tray, then looked at his watch and shook his head. "Didn't someone bring me dinner a few hours ago? I told them I wasn't hungry."

"Yes," Hallie said. "My aunts were here. But you didn't eat. I thought maybe you didn't care for the food, so I brought you something else." She walked past him into the room and placed the tray on the small table in the dining nook.

He stood at the door and watched her as she arranged the meal on the table. "I'm not hungry now, Miss Tyler," he said.

"But you have to eat, Mr. Tristan," Hallie protested.

"Just have a little something. You look a little . . . pale . . . I mean, a little exhausted." She bit her bottom lip, certain now that she'd insulted him as well as interrupted him.

He raised a dark eyebrow and studied her astutely. "I'm fine, Miss Tyler. There's no need to worry about me."

Hallie forced a smile. "Well, I've brought you a sandwich and some pie. Why don't you sit down and eat?"

Tris frowned. "I'm not hungry," he repeated. "In fact, I was right in the middle of something when you knocked and I'd like to get back to it . . . if you don't mind."

Good grief, he was certainly anxious to get rid of her. But she wasn't about to leave until she'd proved her point to her aunts. "You paid for a room that includes dinner," Hallie said stubbornly. "It would be a shame not to eat."

"I'll eat later," he said in an equally intractable voice.

"Just try a little something."

Tris crossed his arms over his chest, an irritated expression suffusing his face. "I sense that you really didn't come here to offer me dinner, Miss Tyler. Was there something else you wanted?"

Hallie felt a flush creep up her cheeks at the obvious implication in his words. He thought she'd come here to flirt with him! Like some randy chambermaid in a bad French farce! Of all the arrogant, egotistical, overbearing— But instead of a smirking countenance, he watched her with an open, inquiring expression.

Hallie swallowed her anger and tried to maintain a cool expression. "I don't know what you mean," she said. "I'm simply trying to make your stay here as comfortable as possible."

"Your aunts took care of that already," he said. He slowly approached and she felt a shiver run down her spine as he came closer. She could almost feel an unseen power emanate from his body. She clenched her hands in front of her and watched him warily.

If he really wanted the truth, she'd tell him the real reason she'd come—to prove to her crazy aunts that he wasn't a vampire. But she'd much prefer that he thought she'd come to f. t rather than to question his eating habits.

Nervously, she turned and picked up a glass of milk from the tray and dropped it on the table, sending a geyser shooting up so high it hit her in the face. Hallie calmly wiped the milk off her nose, then turned to him. "If . . . if you need anything else, Mr. Tristan, just call the house," she said. "Enjoy your dinner."

With that, she turned on her heel and hurried toward the door. He pulled it open before her and she walked through. She heard the door close behind her and she cursed softly.

She stopped twenty feet from the cottage, then turned back, knowing a good innkeeper would return and apologize for the intrusion. But she wasn't about to apologize for *his* rude behavior. Instead, Hallie kept to the shadows of the trees and crept up close to the window, then peered in.

Edward Tristan stood over the table and stared down at the meal she'd brought him. He reached out and picked up one half of the sandwich and examined it. She held her breath, waiting for him to take a bite. But he tossed it back on the plate. She didn't wait to see more.

Prudence and Patience were waiting for her when she returned to the kitchen. "Well?" Patience said.

"He wasn't hungry," Hallie snapped.

"There it is," Prudence said. "We told you, dear."

"He is not a vampire!" Hallie practically growled through clenched teeth.

He's an incredibly gorgeous man, she mused. A little distracted and aloof, but gorgeous nonetheless. She had to admit, if there actually were vampires, he might make a good one with those dark features and that brooding manner. But Hallie knew vampires didn't exist.

Now if she could only write Mr. Tristan off as easily.

TRISTAN STARED at the closed door for a long time, then frowned and turned away. He walked back to the desk and glanced down at his computer, trying to regain his train of thought. But words and characters no longer filled his mind as they had just minutes before. They had all been replaced by a tantalizing image of Hallie Tyler.

He cursed softly, then reached out and hit a series of commands to back up his work. He'd been working on his manuscript almost nonstop for the past three nights, the story flowing out of his mind fully formed. All his other books had been born from hard labor, word by word, paragraph by paragraph, but not this one. It was almost like a gift from the gods.

He slowly read the page he'd just finished. He had reached the point in the story where the heroine first comes face-to-face with the hero, a restless vampire anxious to shed his immortality and live his life as a mortal. The words were lush with description, every sentence filled with a disturbing sensuality and an uneasy sexual tension between the two characters. He'd already come up with a title. *Wicked Ways*.

He closed his eyes and stretched his arms above his head, then stood without moving, allowing his thoughts to wander. Hallie really was the most beautiful woman he'd ever met. Not beautiful in a sensational way, but in a fresh, innocent, almost untouched way. How many times had his thoughts turned to her over the past three days? He had obsessed over the perfection of her skin, the dewy softness of her lips and the silky shine of her dark hair until he could reproduce each on the page.

Tris groaned inwardly. Maybe it hadn't been such a good idea to base his heroine on a real woman. When he wasn't thinking about the fictional Hallie, he was thinking about the real one. A woman he'd practically thrown out of the coach house just a few minutes ago.

He knew he'd confused her. She'd expected him to be kind, or at least cordial. But when he worked, his mind blocked out all else but the world of his characters. He became self-absorbed, distracted. He should have taken time out to talk to her, but truth be told, he wasn't quite sure what to say.

In just a few short days he'd almost fallen in love with the fictional woman on the page. Face-to-face with her real-life inspiration, he felt as if he knew her as well— almost intimately. Yet he didn't know Hallie Tyler at all.

Was the niggling attraction he felt when he looked at her real? Or was it simply a side effect left over from her fictional counterpart? Suddenly he needed to know for sure. Tris flipped off his computer, grabbed his coat from the back of the sofa and pulled it on.

The night air was crisp and smelled of the sea. Tris strode toward the inn, holding a lantern in front of him to mark the path. As the trees thinned, he saw the house ablaze with light from every multipaned window. He hesitated for a moment, wondering how many of the guests were still up and about.

A movement at the edge of the bluff caught his eye and he turned to see Hallie's form outlined against the sea by the light from the house. She looked so forlorn, standing alone on the bluff, the brisk sea air whipping through her hair and buffeting her slender body.

Suddenly she turned and stared at the inn, her hands clutched to her chest. He quickly lowered the flame on the lantern. At first he thought she'd seen him, but then he realized he was well hidden in the shadows of an old oak, outside the spill of light from the porch. He wanted her to stay there, a perfect silhouette against the rising moon, a picture for him to savor without thought or word.

He had to admit, she was a beautiful woman, a woman who had the capacity to fascinate him with just one winsome smile. If she'd come into his life at another time he might have pursued her, but now was not the right time. He had a book to write and precious little time to do it. Wooing a woman like Hallie would not fit into his schedule. Besides, he sensed she was not the type of woman to settle for a brief, no-strings affair. And that was all Tristan had ever been able to offer.

She slowly walked across the lawn and he waited as she approached the porch, ready to let her pass without a word. But at the last instant he reached out of the shadows and gently touched her shoulder.

Hallie spun around and a strangled scream escaped her throat. Wide-eyed, she stared up at him.

"Have I frightened you?" Tris asked.

"Wh-what are you doing sneaking up on me like that?" Hallie cried, the color high in her pretty cheeks, her hair gilded gold by the porch light.

He couldn't help but move his hand from her shoulder to her cheek, to see if her skin was truly as soft as it looked. He brushed his knuckles against her jaw, then pulled his hand away. "I've been waiting for you," he said, staring down into her bright eyes.

"What for?" she asked.

"I wanted to apologize for being so abrupt," he said softly. "I got the impression that you were angry with me. Were you angry, Hallie?"

She scoffed. "Now it's Hallie," she said. "Just a few minutes ago it was Miss Tyler."

Tristan shrugged. He didn't remember much of what was said at the coach house. "Sometimes I become preoccupied with my thoughts. When I'm disturbed I often behave without a care for other's feelings. I didn't mean to seem ungrateful, Hallie. The meal was delicious."

"You ate it?" she asked, disbelief coloring her voice.

He chuckled. "Of course I did."

Hallie smiled in satisfaction and Tris felt his blood warm. Lord, she was pretty when she smiled. Prettier than any heroine he might fabricate in his mind.

"My aunts will be happy to hear that," she said.

"And why is that?" he asked, his gaze fixed on her lush mouth.

"Because they—" She hesitated for a moment. "Because they made the pie," she finally said.

"Well, tell them the cherry pie was quite good," he murmured.

Hallie blinked in surprise. "Apple pie," she corrected, her eyes widening slightly.

"What?" Tris asked, his attention moving from her mouth back to their conversation.

"The pie," she said. "It was apple, not cherry."

He cleared his throat, realizing why he'd said cherry. Her lips reminded him of sweet red cherries. "It was very good, nonetheless."

She stood in the light of the porch and stared up at him, an odd expression on her face, half confusion, half apprehension. If he didn't know better, he'd think she was frightened. For a long time they didn't speak, then she drew a sharp breath. "Was there something else you needed, Mr. Tristan?"

"Tris," he reminded her.

"Tris," she repeated uneasily.

"Actually, I was hoping you might show me where your Uncle Nicholas is buried."

She seemed taken aback by his request. "Now? But it's dark out," she said.

Tris grinned. "What better time to visit a cemetery?" he countered.

"Uncle Nicholas isn't buried in the Episcopal Cemetery," Hallie replied. "He's buried in a small family plot about fifty yards to the north of the church cemetery. My great-great-uncle and the church parted ways early on in his life. It really would be better to go during the day."

"But I'd prefer to see it at night," Tris said. He grabbed the lantern that he'd used to find his way to the inn and turned up the flame. "Come on. There's nothing to be frightened of. I promise I'll protect you." His voice was teasing, but deep down he wondered at the strange surge of protectiveness he felt whenever he was around Hallie.

Her gaze snapped up to his. "I'm not frightened," she said. "Why would you think I'd be frightened?"

"Your uncle was a vampire," Tris said.

"I don't believe in vampires," Hallie replied. "And neither do you."

"Then we needn't be frightened. Let's be off, Hallie Tyler. Ghosts and goblins await."

Tris stuck out his arm and Hallie smiled reluctantly, then slipped her hand through his bent elbow. Her touch was casual, but it sent a rush of warmth coursing through his bloodstream.

"I thought you weren't one of those vampire chasers," she said.

"I'm not," Tris replied. "I'm merely interested in the local history. This is a wonderful little village you have here and I want to know more about it." For Tris, everything was fodder for his book, including Egg Harbor and its residents—dead and alive.

"It *is* wonderful," Hallie said wistfully. "I just hope it stays that way."

"Why wouldn't it?"

She clutched his arm more tightly against her and stared off into the darkness. "There are people in Egg Harbor who are thrilled with the recent tourism boom. And they're willing to do anything to see that it continues. I'm just as determined to see that it stops."

They walked silently down the curving road toward the village, Tris holding the lantern up high. The wavering light cast eerie shadows on the trees. Night sounds ebbed and flowed out of the woods that surrounded them and the wind rustled the leaves, sometimes whipping them up into little whirlwinds in front of them.

Tris felt Hallie's hand grip his forearm and he looked down at her and smiled. He bent close to her ear. "Don't worry," he whispered, "I've got a wooden stake in my pocket, just in case."

"I'm not scared," Hallie said.

They came to a bend in the road and Hallie pointed to the right. "The family plot is right behind the cemetery. There's a little path through the trees and brush. My aunts usually tend to it so it doesn't get overgrown."

Tris raised the lantern and walked along the edge of the Episcopal graveyard, pulling Hallie along behind him. She stumbled slightly and he stopped. "Are you all right?" he asked.

She nodded, her eyes wide. "Of course," she said. "I used to come out here all the time when I was a kid. My friends and I used to tell spooky stories and scare ourselves silly."

The Tyler family plot, surrounded by a high brick wall and protected by an iron gate, was hidden in the trees. The grass and leaves around the entrance were well trampled and Tris suspected that some of the vampire watchers had come to take a look.

Hallie walked up to the wall and with practiced movements carefully removed a loose brick and pulled out an ancient key. "I—I haven't been inside for quite a while," she said as she pushed the key into the lock. The gate sprang open on creaking hinges and she gingerly stepped through.

She glanced around, then pointed. "Uncle Nicholas is buried over there in the corner," she said, her voice trembling slightly.

Tris grabbed her hand again and tugged her along with him. The lantern light reflected off the old, weatherworn markers as they made their way to the far corner of the plot.

"Nicholas Tyler," Hallie said, reading his name off the gravestone. "Here he is."

Tris knelt down and skimmed his hand over the dried leaves and brown grass mounded over the grave. "What do you know of him?" he asked, glancing up at her.

She shrugged. "Not much," Hallie replied. "He was a bit of a black sheep. Wasn't interested in the family business. Rumor has it he liked wine, women and song."

Tris squinted and held the lantern closer. "Look at this," he said, pointing to a spot of loose dirt near the headstone.

Hallie bent down beside him. "What is it?"

"Little holes."

"Squirrels?" she asked.

"Not if you believe in vampires. That's one of the signs. Finger-size holes near the grave."

She jumped back and landed on her backside, then scrambled away from the grave. "How do you know this?"

"I've been doing some reading," Tris replied, studying the holes further. The truth be told, he'd been doing a lot more than that. This whole Tyler family vampire legend had been too fascinating to resist. He'd tapped into the Internet and downloaded reams of information about the undead onto his laptop.

"I—I think we should leave," she said.

Tris glanced over his shoulder. "You're not frightened, are you?"

"I'm getting there," Hallie said.

Reaching down, Tris plucked a piece of fabric from beneath a pile of leaves. "Here's something else," he said. He handed Hallie the fabric, then moved the lantern closer to examine it. "It looks like it's torn from an old garment."

"There's a button attached," she murmured, fingering it carefully. "It looks like..." She drew a shaky breath. "Scrimshaw. I think it's made of whalebone. There's a designed carved into it. I—I've seen these kinds of buttons before," she said.

"Where?" Tris asked.

She pressed the fabric back into his hand as if she couldn't stand to touch it. "In the attic of the inn. We have some old clothing from the turn of the century, packed away in trunks. They've got whalebone buttons just like this." Hallie got to her feet. "I think we should leave," she repeated more emphatically.

"Wait," Tris said. "We should look for more clues."

"I don't believe in vampires," she shouted over her shoulder.

"Hallie," he called. "Come on. Don't leave." He grabbed the lantern and hurried after her, catching up just as she reached the iron gate. Tris grabbed her arm and spun her around.

She gazed up at him, her eyes wide. "I don't like this," she said.

He reached up and placed his palm against her cheek, staring down into her eyes. Slowly, he bent toward her, imagining the feel of her mouth against his. But at the last second she pulled back, stepping away from him.

"I—I have to get back to the inn," she said.

"All right," Tris replied. "Let's go."

She didn't wait for Tris, but hurried through the gate of the graveyard, locking it the instant Tris stepped through. Their walk back was brisk, nearly a jog. If Tristan didn't know better, he would have thought she was running away from something.

When she said a hasty good-night on the front porch of the inn and slipped through the door without a backward glance, Tris was *certain* she was frightened of something. The strange thing was, he didn't think it was vampires that she was running from.

In fact, if his guess was right, Hallie Tyler was running from him.

THE VILLAGE HALL sat on a narrow spit of land near the waterfront. The white clapboard building had been erected in the late eighteen hundreds after the lumber and shipping industry brought people to the little harbor town.

The hall was crowded with people when Hallie arrived. The monthly village board meeting was a major social event, not because of the politics involved, but because of the free food that the Egg Harbor Ladies' League provided afterward. Every bachelor in need of a home-cooked meal considered it his patriotic duty to add his vote to the proceedings and his appetite to the potluck.

Hallie was usually one of the only women in the audience. The women in town found it odd that she preferred the politics of the meeting to the potluck. But then, most of the townsfolk considered her odd. She been an outspoken opponent of any and all development plans for the village, a view that hadn't made her many friends around town.

Hallie found an empty chair next to Roland Wilson, the town's postmaster. He nodded to her, then turned his attention to the five men seated at the long table in the front of the hall. Hallie knew all five. She'd been on opposite sides of nearly every issue with the board and tonight would probably be no different. Whether they chose to listen to her or not, she would have her say.

"All right, all right," Silas Pemberton shouted, rapping his gavel on the table. "Settle in now. Let's get this meeting started so we can all enjoy the tasty repast that the ladies have prepared for us."

The audience broke into a round of applause and Silas waved his hands in a gesture for quiet. The man cut an imposing figure. Silas was tall and barrel-chested with a wild shock of white hair. He had served as the town's mayor for nearly a quarter century and had run unopposed for all of that time, until last year. Silas didn't take kindly to opposition.

"On agreement from the rest of the board members—Abner, Jonah, Sam, and Ephriam—we're going to dispense with the readin' of the minutes and table our usual agenda of discussing our sewage problems and the new garbage truck we wanna buy. We're going to get right to the business of tourism. Jonah has a report."

Jonah McCabe, a middle-aged man, tall and skinny as a lodgepole pine, stood and cleared his throat. As he spoke, his Adam's apple bobbed above his starched white collar. "We got ourselves a major influx of tourists here in town due to the presence of a member of the vampire species up there at the Widder's Walk Inn."

Everyone in the room turned to look at Hallie and she groaned. This was worse than she'd anticipated. The revival of the Tyler family legend was all Silas Pemberton needed to push his tourism agenda. And he'd been aided and abetted by her very own relatives—Patience and Prudence.

"Now, these vampire folks have been spendin' a lot of money here in town," Jonah continued, "and I think we got to come up with a plan to keep these folks coming back. Ephriam's got some suggestions he worked up."

Ephriam Whitley didn't bother to stand, preferring to keep his considerable bulk in the small folding chair. "I think we ought to turn Egg Harbor into the vampire capital of the world," Ephriam stated grandly. Ephriam was a man with big ideas, ideas that matched his size and his rather large ego. "We got small towns all over the United States with their own claim to fame. You got the Turnip Capital, the Cranberry Capital, even the Cowpie Capital. I believe that if we don't grab ourselves our own piece of the pie, someone else will snatch it right off our plate. Now, is there any discussion or can we vote on this right away?"

"What do ya have in mind there, Ephriam?" someone shouted from the audience.

Ephriam scratched his double chin and pondered the question for a long moment. "Well, I propose we throw ourselves a Vampire Festival. We start bringing people into town and Egg Harbor'll be just like all them other towns up and down the coast. Heck, before long, we could have ourselves a regular fast-food restaurant move in here."

Hallie couldn't keep quiet any longer and jumped out of her chair. "Now, wait a minute," she cried. "I don't think you realize what tourism will do to this town!"

Silas peered at her through his reading glasses. "Who is that?" he asked.

"Hallie Tyler," she replied.

"Well, you just sit yourself down there, little lady. Ephriam's giving his report."

"Ephriam called for discussion and I have something to say," Hallie replied.

Ephriam turned to Abner Cromwell, the town clerk. "Do we have to let her speak? Once she gets started you know it ain't going to be easy to put a cork in her."

Abner shook his head solemnly, then went back to chewing on the stem of his pipe.

"According to *Robert's Rules of Order*, you have to recognize me!" Hallie cried. Though she wasn't sure on that point, she did know that not one board member had read *Robert's Rules*. The last time she'd been in Abner's office, the little book had been jammed under a wobbly desk leg.

Silas raised a bushy white brow and gave her an irritated glare. "We all recognize you. You're Hallie Tyler and you live up at the Widow's Walk. Now let's get back to our discussion. Anyone else have something more pertinent to say regarding Ephriam's report?"

"This isn't a discussion if you won't let me speak freely," she countered.

Silas pointed a crooked finger at her. "We all know what you have to say, Hallie Tyler, and we don't want to hear it. So to save time, let's just skip over *your* say in this matter and get right to what *we* have to say."

"But I have something important—"

"We all know you're still stinging from your recent defeat in the mayoral election," Abner interrupted. The clerk hooked his thumbs under his suspenders and puffed out his chest. "I told you not to run against Silas, little lady. Your liberal viewpoints will only get you in trouble."

Hallie gasped. "I am *not* still stinging," she shouted. "I never stung in the first place. And I am not your *little* lady. I own a business in this town and I have a right to my opinion."

Ephriam Whitley slapped his palms on the table. "You're just worried that if we get our town some tourists, you might get yourself some competition for your inn. Maybe one of them big hotel chains will decide to build us a proper hotel with satellite TV and them vibrating beds."

Hallie drew herself up to her full five-foot-five-inch height, her spine stiff with indignation. "I'm worried that your ill-conceived plan will ruin this town, a town that my great-great-grandfather founded. Have any of you ever walked down the streets of Camden at the height of tourist season? The town belongs to strangers. The townspeople are only there to fetch and carry."

"Yeah, but we'd get paid real good for fetchin' and carryin'," Jonah said. "Fishing's been mighty poor over the past few years. We got to make our living somehow. Tourists make a town rich."

"They also go away in the winter. What do you all expect to do for a living from October through April?"

"We can make plenty in the summer months," Ephriam said.

"You're all just willing to sell this town to the highest bidder—in this case, a bunch of vampire fanatics." Hallie shook her head in disgust. "You have no idea what this will do to Egg Harbor."

"I don't know why you're all in a huff, Hallie Tyler. It's your great-great-uncle Nicholas Tyler who started all this," Silas said.

"Nicholas Tyler was *not* a vampire," Hallie said. "That's simply a silly rumor that someone started."

"Airing your family's dirty laundry can be an embarrassing proposition," Jonah commented. "But I wouldn't feel too bad about old Nick. He's going to put Egg Harbor on the map."

"He's my uncle," Hallie said. "And I refuse to let you use him, or his name, in this ridiculous plan."

Silas gave her a dubious look. "The way I see it, Hallie Tyler, old Nicholas is what you'd call a community asset. He belongs to all of us and if we want to build a statue of him in the village square, there ain't nothin' you can do to stop us. Now, are you through being recognized, or do you have something else you want to carp about?"

Hallie cursed silently, knowing that no matter how long she talked, she'd find no support for her views. "I will not be a part of this," she said, pushing through the row until she reached the aisle. "You won't get my support on this plan, Silas Pemberton, and you'll never get me to say that vampires are anything more than a figment of someone's imagination."

"We don't need your support, missy," Silas called as she shoved open the door.

Hallie strode down the main street of Egg Harbor, her temper ready to explode. How could they not realize what they had here? The town was untouched, pristine in its beauty. Egg Harbor was one of the few villages left on the coast that hadn't been overrun with tacky T-shirt shops and touristy restaurants.

Instead, Egg Harbor was filled with perfect whitewashed clapboard houses and old brick buildings that dated back to the turn of the century, pretty streets shaded with tall maple and oak trees, and a harbor that sparkled with clean, clear water. People knew each other and cared for their neighbors, and though life was sometimes hard on the rocky coast of Maine, Egg Harbor had always survived.

The guests that stayed at her inn appreciated the unspoiled beauty. Many of them kept their love for Egg Harbor a closely held secret, knowing that once more tourists came, the charming little town would be ruined. And Hallie had done her part, turning down her share of reservations and only taking the guests she needed to make a living.

But now everything she'd come to love about Egg Harbor was at risk. Her great-great-grandfather had put his heart into the town and she wasn't about to let Silas Pemberton tear it apart.

There had to be a way to stop him. But how? She was only one person in this town, a person no one bothered to listen to.

But she *was* the lady with the vampire. And if she could prove that her uncle Nicholas had died and stayed dead, then the Vampire Festival would be exposed as a sham.

The sun was down when she reached the inn, but she had no trouble finding her way. She knew every inch of Egg Harbor and her property by heart. A light over the door bathed the porch in a golden glow, making the inn look cozy and inviting. But she wasn't ready to face Patience and Prudence right now.

Instead she walked to the edge of the bluff and stood silently, her gaze fixed on the tiny town below. How could she make them understand what this place meant to her? She'd grown to love her life here, the fresh salt air and clear blue skies, the solitude and the quiet.

Hallie closed her eyes and tipped her head back, drawing deeply of the damp night air. She'd find a way to win this fight. She had to, for her life depended on it.

3

HALLIE RAPPED on the door of the coach house, then glanced down at the note she had clutched in her hand. *Please see Mr. Tristan immediately.* One of the aunts had left it tacked to the bulletin board next to the phone and she'd seen it when she'd returned from the town meeting. Tacked alongside the note was a tarnished silver bell suspended on a grosgrain ribbon, no doubt another one of the Sisters' charms to ward off vampires.

At first, she'd ignored the note—and the bell. She didn't want to see Mr. Tristan. Not immediately, not later, not ever again. After their encounter in the cemetery, it had become blatantly clear to her that she had no self-control when it came to the man. And she sensed that he planned to take advantage of that fact. Good grief, if she hadn't pulled away, he probably would have kissed her right there amid the tombstones!

The coach house door swung open in front of her and she looked up to find Tristan standing in front of her. "It's about time you got here," he grumbled. He turned away from her, leaving Hallie standing there in the doorway, wondering what she was about to walk into. She'd never met a man quite as mercurial as Edward Tristan. One moment he was snapping at her impatiently and the next he was charming her socks off.

She watched him pace the room restlessly. He looked like he hadn't slept in days and she sensed he was very near to losing his temper. "Is there a problem?" she asked, stepping inside and closing the door behind her.

"It's that damn sink in the bathroom. It's dripping and driving me half mad. You have to fix it," Tris said. "Right away."

Hallie bristled at his demanding tone and forced a polite smile. "I'll see what I can do." She walked through the great room to the adjoining bathroom, then flipped on the light. The scent of his cologne touched her nose and she took a long breath and closed her eyes for a moment, savoring the spicy scent she'd remembered so well from the previous night.

"You can fix it, can't you?"

Hallie jumped at the sound of his voice, so close she could feel his warm breath on the nape of her neck. She stepped up to the sink, then turned the water on and off several times, trying to still the tremble in her hands. She turned around and faced him. "It looks like the washer on the cold water faucet needs to be replaced."

"Is that serious?"

"Not very."

A look of relief suffused his face. "And you'll fix it now?"

Hallie sighed. "My toolbox is in the spare bedroom. Why don't you go get it, while I turn off the water?" She watched him leave, then took off her jacket and sat down on the floor in front of the pedestal sink. Twisting herself around the base of the sink, she reached back and attempted to turn the valves from the water supply. But one of the valves had frozen tight and no matter how much effort she put into it, it refused to turn.

Hallie looked up as Tris returned to the bathroom, her toolbox in his hand. "Can you hand me the vise grips?" she asked.

Tris set the toolbox on the floor and opened it. "Which one would be the vise grips?"

"It looks kind of like a pipe wrench with a spring handle."

Tris stared down into the contents of the toolbox as if he hadn't a clue as to what she wanted. He plucked out a pair of pliers and then a crescent wrench. Hallie sighed and crawled out from under the sink. She dug through the tools until she found what she wanted. She held them up in front of Tris's nose. "Vise grips," she said.

He raised a sardonic brow. "How enlightening," he said dryly. "I don't think I could have lived a day longer without such vital knowledge."

Hallie couldn't help but smile. "I take it you don't have your own tools at home? I thought all men had tools."

"I have a building superintendent and he has tools," Tris replied. "Lots of tools. It's a much better arrangement. I phone him, he brings his tools over, and he fixes everything."

Hallie tried again to get some leverage on the valve, but it still wouldn't turn. She cursed softly. "It's stuck. I can't turn the water off."

He peered up at the sink, then back at her. "The water *is* off."

"I mean the water line. I have to turn it off before I can replace the washer in the faucet. Unless you'd like to take an impromptu shower."

He cocked his eyebrow up and grinned. "Now there's something my super never offered." Tris sat down on the floor next to her and reached past her to the wall behind the sink. "Let me try." His back pressed against her breasts and a warm flood of sensation seeped through her body. She tried to push away, but the side of the whirlpool tub prevented her retreat, allowing no escape from his touch.

"Is this it?" he murmured, stretching to lie across her lap.

Hallie cleared her throat nervously and reached behind the sink. His fingers laced through hers and he wrapped her hand around the valve. "Yes," she said, her voice cracking. "Try to turn that counterclockwise." He twisted again in her lap and she snatched her hand back, feeling as if she'd been scalded by his touch.

As he worked, her gaze drifted along his lean torso to his narrow hips and long legs. She hadn't been this close to a man in ages and she'd forgotten the effect it could have on her senses, the sudden desire that pulsed deep inside her core.

She wanted to touch him, to move her palms over his body, to feel every inch of hard flesh and unforgiving muscle. Her eyes fixed on his belly, where his sweater had pulled from the waistband of his jeans, and she allowed her imagination to follow the dusting of hair that disappeared beneath the top button. With unabashed curiosity, she let her gaze drop lower, to the contours hidden behind the denim.

She closed her eyes and drew a fortifying breath, trying to halt the unbidden fantasies that raced through her mind. He shifted against her again, sending an-

other surge of sensation through her limbs, and she bit
her bottom lip to keep from moaning out loud.

"Hallie?"

Her eyes snapped open and she found him gazing up
at her, an odd smile quirking the corners of his mouth.

"Are you all right?"

Hallie cleared her throat and blinked hard. Her
cheeks warmed beneath his curious perusal and she
nodded. "Did you fix it?"

He crawled off her lap and wiped his hands on his
thighs. "It's off. I think."

Hallie quickly got to her feet, avoiding his eyes. She
flipped on both faucets and watched as a small stream
of water dribbled out, then died. "Thank you," she said
breathlessly.

He chuckled, then levered himself up and took a seat
on the edge of the whirlpool. "I guess it sometimes pays
to have a man around."

She gave him a sideways glance, her eyes wide. Had
he read her thoughts? Had he sensed what his touch had
done to her? She groaned inwardly, then bent to busy
herself with rearranging her toolbox.

"Is there anything else I can do to help?"

Hallie shook her head. "You've done quite enough
already," she muttered. "I think I can handle it from
here."

But much to Hallie's consternation, Tris didn't take
her comment as an invitation to leave. Instead, he continued to watch her, perched on the edge of the tub. She
could feel his eyes on her as she worked, following her
every move, lazily drifting along her body until she
wanted to crawl inside the shower stall and shut the
door behind her.

"You amaze me, Hallie," he murmured.

"Why is that?"

"I've never met anyone quite like you. You're very independent."

"I've had to learn to take care of things around here on my own," she said.

"Do you ever get lonely?"

His question took her by surprise. She glanced over her shoulder to find him studying her intently. She couldn't lie to him. She sensed he would know that she wasn't speaking the truth. "Sometimes," she admitted. "But I usually find plenty to keep me busy. I have my aunts. And there are always people around, guests at the inn."

"I'm surprised that you're still alone," he commented.

"I told you, I'm not alone. I have my aunts."

He met her gaze. "That's not what I meant."

"What *did* you mean?" she asked, a hint of defensiveness in her voice.

"Have you ever been in love?"

She paused for a moment, not sure whether she should answer such a blunt and personal question. But Tris had a way of speaking to her, exerting some strange power over her and lulling her into a sense of security, that she couldn't help but reply to his question.

"Once," she replied. "His name was Jonathan and I was supposed to marry him. After my mother died, I inherited the house. I wanted to come back here to live, but he wouldn't consider it. He liked the city and felt living in Egg Harbor just wasn't for him. I knew he was right. Small-town life isn't for everyone. But I had to come back. Something inside me was connected to this place and I just couldn't sell it."

"And what about now? What if you had to choose again? Would you make the same choice?"

She nodded. "I would. This is my home. It's all I have left of my family. I belong here." She tossed her wrench back into her toolbox and closed the top. "There. I think that should take care of the drippy faucet. Your peace and quiet has been restored."

Hallie bent to pick up the toolbox, but Tris quickly stood, then bent and covered her hand with his. For a long moment she didn't move, just stared at his fingers.

"Let me get it for you," he said, his words soft against her temple. "It's heavy."

Hallie slowly straightened, clutching her hands in front of her and trying to rub the tingling numbness from her fingertips. "I—I'd better go," she murmured. "I've got a lot of work to do up at the house."

He grabbed her hand as she moved to make her escape. She turned and looked up at him, then found herself nearly overwhelmed by the intensity that burned deep in his eyes.

"Thank you," he said, giving her hand a squeeze.

"Th-that's what I'm here for," Hallie replied, dragging her gaze from his. With that, she hurried to the door, afraid to look back.

Once outside, Hallie stumbled down the path to the inn. Her mind whirled with confusion as she flung open the back door then slammed it shut behind her. She pressed her palm to her chest and tried to catch her breath.

She had been right to be wary of Mr. Edward Tristan! The man definitely wanted something from her. Hallie pinched her eyes shut and tried to rid herself of the memory of his body touching hers, of the incredible power he seemed to exert over her.

Oh, yes. He wanted something. She just wasn't sure what it was.

TRIS SLID ONTO a stool at Earl's Diner and snatched a menu from the clip behind the catsup bottle. The diner, located on Egg Harbor's main street, was empty, silent except for an occasional muttered curse from the heavy-set proprietor behind the worn Formica-topped counter.

"Damned thing," he said, whacking an ornate espresso machine with a spatula. "I told her I didn't want this blasted contraption. 'Earl,' she says, 'we got to get with the times.' Get with the times, my big toe!"

He glared at the machine, arms akimbo. Suddenly the espresso maker hissed and Earl jumped back, his wide eyes watching the machine suspiciously. "What the hell is that?" He turned to Tris and gave him a questioning look.

"I think it's supposed to make that noise," Tris said. They both watched as a stream of rich, dark espresso bubbled out of the machine into a small glass pot.

"Well, now, there's a fine machine!" Earl said in amazement, peering more closely at the operation. "It works. You like this espresso coffee?"

Tris shrugged. "Sure. I wouldn't mind an espresso. I've got a long night ahead of me and I could use the caffeine. Maybe you could add a little steamed milk?"

"Steamed milk?" Earl snatched up the instruction manual and skimmed the directions, then methodically prepared the milk. Ten minutes later, after a considerable amount of cursing, he presented Tris with a brimming coffee mug emblazoned with the Earl's Diner logo.

"Go ahead," he said. "Give 'er a try. Tell me what you think."

Tris took a sip of the fragrant brew and smiled. "It's good," he said.

A wide smile split Earl's florid face and he clapped his hands. "Never thought I'd see the day I'd go trendy, but the wife says all these tourists are gonna demand this fancy stuff. You want another? I got all these flavors I can mix in."

Tris nodded and silently sipped at his coffee. The second cup appeared in front of him, this time with perfectly frothed milk, a shot of chocolate syrup and a dusting of cocoa powder. "Not bad for an old hash slinger, eh?" Earl said. "The book says that there's a mocha."

Tris picked up the mocha and took a taste. "Not bad," he replied. "Just like you get in New York City."

Earl's chest puffed with pride. "You from New York?"

Tris nodded, reluctant to offer any more information.

"You stayin' up at the Widow's Walk?"

Tris set his cup down and idly turned it in the saucer, carefully composing his answer. He'd learned to be suspicious of strangers, constantly guessing at their motives and reluctant to answer any questions, even the most benign. He preferred to be the one doing the asking—all in the name of research, of course. "I'm staying in the coach house. I thought I wouldn't have trouble finding a room, but with all this vampire business, the inn was full when I arrived. I was hoping for some peace and quiet."

"If you came looking for quiet," Earl said, "Hallie's is the place for you. There's no better innkeeper on the coast of Maine. She takes real good care of her guests."

"She's quite a woman," Tris commented with a wry grin.

Earl raised a bushy white eyebrow and nodded. "You've noticed. You and every other single man in town."

"Then she has a lot of . . ." Tris searched for an appropriate word.

"Suitors?" Earl asked. "Nah. Most men just admire her from afar. She is a pretty little thing. But Hallie doesn't let folks get too close. She keeps to herself, except when she's got an opinion to offer, and then it's best to run the other way. She holds some rather unpopular views on tourism and I think that sets a few folks on edge."

"You'd think she'd want more tourists," Tris commented. "It would certainly be better for business. And it would make her life more secure."

"Most folks can't figure Hallie out, but I've watched the girl grow up. I knew her folks. Sometimes I think she's right to want Egg Harbor to stay the same. She ran for mayor last year on that very platform. Only got five percent of the vote though."

"I guess bucking progress is a thankless job," Tris said.

"That doesn't stop Hallie from tryin'. She's been fighting development plans from the start, ever since she came back here from Boston. Her folks had her late in life and they raised her to be a real stubborn little cuss. She's the last of the Tyler line, except for the Sisters, of course. She was forced to turn the Tyler place into an inn after both her parents passed on, but that doesn't stop her from wantin' to keep the city folks out."

"City folks?"

"Yeah, she thinks if one hotshot celebrity comes, they'll all come. They'll buy up the property and make it too expensive for the folks in town to stay. I suppose she wasn't too happy to see you come."

Tris's gaze snapped up to meet Earl's. "Why is that?"

Earl shrugged. "'Cause you're famous," he replied matter-of-factly. "You are Tristan Montgomery, aren't you? I recognized you right off, from the picture on the back of your books."

Tris took a long breath, then slowly exhaled. "I was hoping I wouldn't be recognized. You're the first."

"Folks around here don't do much pleasure reading," he explained. "Me, I put in some pretty lonely nights here. I like reading."

"Why do you stay open if you don't have customers?"

"I guess I'm just a night person. And once in a while, I have some company. You stopped by, didn't you?"

Tris smiled. "I'm a night person, too. It's when I do my best work."

Earl chuckled. "You, me, and old Nick Tyler, the town vampire."

"You won't tell anyone who I am, will you?" Tris asked.

"Not if you don't want me to. You've got a right to your privacy. Does Hallie know?"

Tris shook his head. "I feel pretty silly announcing who I am. It seems a little narcissistic. After what you told me, she might just decide to put me out on the street if she finds out."

"I'm sure if you just sweet talked her a little, she'd be happy to let you stay," Earl replied.

Sweet talk. Is that what he was doing with Hallie? Leading her on, toying with her emotions, playing games with her heart? He hadn't come to Egg Harbor looking for female companionship. He usually left that to the time in between books, days when he could forget his writing and concentrate on having a good time.

He knew better than to start something with Hallie. Right now, he didn't have the luxury of time. Yet he couldn't seem to stop himself. Whenever he looked at her, he seemed to find an extra surge of energy, as if her mere presence filled him with a new passion for life.

What did he want from her? Was he simply interested in character research? Or was he interested in the intriguing woman behind the wide green eyes? If Tristan Montgomery knew what was good for him, he'd check out of the Widow's Walk Inn tonight and find another place to stay.

But the Widow's Walk had been good to him so far. He felt comfortable there, and he'd never written better. Tris rubbed his temples and sighed. He'd stay at the Widow's Walk, but he'd do right to stay away from Hallie Tyler. She'd certainly done her damnedest to stay away from him the past few days.

Tris pushed off the stool and reached for his wallet. "Well, I better be on my way. Can you pour me a cup of that coffee to go? In fact, pour me two."

Earl slipped both paper cups into a paper bag, then included a piece of pie. Tris tossed a ten on the counter and, with a wave, headed out the door.

A light fog had descended over the village causing the street lamps to glow in a halo of white light. The clapboard facades of the buildings loomed in the depths of the mist, windows dark, doors locked against the night. His footsteps echoed on the sidewalks and in the distance a dog barked plaintively.

Tris drew a deep breath of the moist air and smiled. Lord, he was beginning to like this place—the silence, the salt-tanged air, the sound of the ocean crashing against the bluffs. He felt comfortable—no, anonymous—here.

And then there was Hallie. The prospect of seeing her was always just a few heartbeats away. It wasn't hard to understand her fascination with this town, or her need to keep it the way it was.

As he climbed the hill to the inn, Tris checked his watch, wondering if Hallie might still be awake. Through the porch window, he saw the glow of a lamp at the front desk and decided to try the door. But when he pushed the door open, the front parlor was silent.

His spirits fell, and it was only then that he realized no matter how much he wanted to stay away from her, he couldn't. He needed to see her, to hear her lilting voice and to look into her tantalizing green eyes just once more before he went back to work. Tris turned to leave, then realized that he wasn't alone after all. Curled in an overstuffed chintz chair in the shadows near the fireplace, Hallie slept, a pen tucked behind her ear and her reservation book clutched against her chest.

Tris crossed the room and slowly knelt beside the chair, staring at her pretty features, so serene and untroubled. He reached out and carefully took the reservation book from her arms and the pen from behind her ear, then pulled a throw from the sofa and draped it over her. She stirred slightly and he held his breath, hoping that she wouldn't wake. He watched her for a long time, drinking in every detail of her face, committing it to memory until he could recall it in an instant.

As if moved by some unknown force, he reached out and brushed his fingertips against her cheek, needing to assure himself that she was real and not just a figment of his imagination. He pulled back, startled by the sensation of warmth that seeped into his fingers until they tingled. Emboldened, he ran his thumb along her lower lip, then softly pushed a strand of dark hair from her temple.

She moved then, moaning quietly, and he froze, his hand hovering over her cheek. Her eyelids fluttered open and she stared at him for a moment, uncomprehending. Her forehead creased into a frown and she opened her mouth to speak.

A surge of desire coursed through his veins as awareness slowly drifted across her face. She didn't move. She seemed almost transfixed, wide-eyed, like a defenseless animal coming face-to-face with a predator. He leaned forward and gently touched his lips to hers.

Tris half expected her to cry out in protest, or at least pull away. But she didn't. Instead her mouth seemed to melt beneath his, her lips soft and moist, and her arms snaked around his neck. He deepened the kiss and cupped her face in his hands, moving her mouth against his. Overwhelmed by the passion she had ignited, he stepped back and looked down into her eyes.

"I think I've wanted to do that since the night I first saw you," he murmured.

Her eyes widened and she blinked in surprise. As if his words had broken a spell, she sat up in her chair and clutched the throw to her chest. "Wh-what are you doing?" she said in a tremulous voice.

He smiled. "I believe I was kissing you, wasn't I?"

She pushed herself up on the arm of the chair, then swung her legs out and scampered behind it, putting several hundred pounds of chintz and stuffing between them. She rubbed her forehead then looked at him in confusion.

Tris reached out for her but she evaded his hand. "Hallie, I'm sorry," he said. "I didn't mean to frighten you."

She shifted uneasily, clutching at the back of the chair, all the while watching him with wary eyes. "You didn't frighten me," she said. "I—I was sleeping."

"Then, what is it? Was I wrong to kiss you?"

She touched her lips. "No," she said softly. "It's just that—never mind. I'm awake now."

Slowly, he straightened and rounded the chair until he stood in front of her, their bodies so close he could feel the warmth radiating from her skin. He could almost hear her quickened pulse. He slipped his hand around the nape of her neck, weaving his fingers through her hair. Then he tugged softly until she was forced to look up at him and meet his gaze directly.

"Would you like me to kiss you again?" he asked in a low voice.

"I—I don't know," she stammered. "I'm not sure."

She touched her tongue to her lips in a nervous gesture, leaving behind a trail of moisture he wanted to kiss away. "Or would you like me to leave?" he asked.

She shook her head, never taking her eyes from his. He bent and kissed her again, long and deep, tasting her fully, until she went soft in his arms and pressed her slender body against his. Desire burned deep in his core, smoldering, ready to flame out of control. But he forced himself to stop, to take a breath and consider just what he was doing.

They barely knew each other, yet he already felt some undeniable connection to her. Was it really her he wanted or was he reacting to the character he'd created?

No! This woman he held in his arms was real, warm and vital, her hair smelling of fresh air and flowers and her lips as sweet as fine wine. And the desire coursing through his body was definitely real.

He gazed down at her flushed cheeks and her moist lips. "I think I'd better go."

She stepped back, slipping out of his arms as easily as she'd come into his embrace. "Perhaps that would be best," she said, refusing to look at him.

Tris strode to the door and picked up the coffee he'd brought from Earl's, then looked back to find her staring after him. He smiled at her. "Sleep well, Hallie. And dream of me."

As Tris walked through the mist to the coach house, he chuckled to himself. He might as well be honest. Staying away from Hallie Tyler would be impossible. When it came to her, he seemed to lose every ounce of his willpower.

Besides, it was probably better to admit defeat and see just what rewards a surrender might bring. If they were anything like the kiss he'd just shared with her, he had a long and interesting stay ahead of him.

HE CAME TO HER in the silken depths of sleep as he had every night since he'd arrived. He stood over her bed, a breeze from the window teasing at his long dark hair. He watched and waited, willing her to reach out to him.

She could feel his eyes on her body, his gaze pushing past the thin gown she wore to the nakedness beneath. She wanted to tear the linen from her damp skin, to catch just a moment's relief from the heat that seemed to surround her.

"Please," she murmured, twisting impatiently beneath his gaze. "Please."

"Then you want me?" he asked, his voice hollow and far away.

"Yes," she breathed. "Yes, I want you."

He reached down and stroked his cool fingers along her forehead. "You can never go back. Never. Once you are mine, you'll be mine forever."

"I understand. Please," she begged. "I don't want to wait any longer."

He smiled then, and slipped into bed beside her, but the mattress didn't move with his weight and she felt nothing more than a presence surrounding her. Confusion clouded her thoughts, drawing her closer to wakefulness, but she pushed it aside, allowing herself to sink more deeply into the dream.

Suddenly he hovered above her, looking down at her with eyes that burned like fire. The breeze blew harder, snapping at his clothes and hair, and sending a chill down her spine. He moaned, his expression one of intense pain and overwhelming passion.

She answered his need by turning her head away from his gaze and offering herself to him. His mouth came down on her neck, his lips cool and moist. She arched against him, wanting to feel his body against hers. But she could feel nothing until—

Hallie bolted upright in bed, her pulse racing and her breath coming in short, desperate gasps. She slapped her hand to her neck, then looked at her fingers in the dim light of the bedroom.

"What is happening to me?" she murmured. She raked her fingers through her hair, then pressed the heels of her hands against her temples and groaned.

Pulling her hands from her face, she glanced furtively around the room. She was alone, yet she could have sworn someone had been in the room with her just moments before. She took a deep breath, rubbed the goose bumps from her arms, then crawled out of bed.

She shook her head and tried to rid her mind of the remnants of the dream. But its aftereffects were still with her. Her skin felt as if it was on fire and she ached with unfulfilled desire.

Hallie grabbed her robe and pulled it on over her nightgown, then headed for the kitchen. She'd make a nice cup of cocoa, or maybe some hot cider. Anything to relax her and put her back to sleep.

But as she walked through the parlor, something drew her to the front windows—a fleeting shadow, a sense of foreboding, she wasn't sure. She peered outside at the exact moment a dark form walked across the front lawn, a lantern in his hand. His features were indistinguishable in the shadows, but she recognized the flowing black trench coat and the long windblown hair, the wide shoulders and the smooth, athletic gait.

Hallie watched Edward Tristan for a moment, then impulsively snatched her jacket from the coat tree beside the door. She yanked her wellies on over her bare feet, then grabbed a flashlight from behind the front desk and headed for the door. If she wanted to know what Edward Tristan was really up to, she'd just have to find out. She'd follow him!

She slipped outside into the windy night, pulling her jacket more tightly around her to ward off the chill. It wasn't difficult to trail along behind Tris. He kept to the middle of the road and his lantern provided a beacon in the dark. She didn't use her flashlight for fear he'd see the light bobbing along behind him.

He turned off the road near the Episcopal cemetery and Hallie followed, careful not to alert him to her presence. Keeping close to the iron fence tangled with vines, she watched as he searched for the path that led to the Tyler family plot.

For a moment, she held back, not wanting to know what he was really doing out here so late at night. But curiosity overcame common sense and she found herself tiptoeing behind him.

He found the key in its niche behind the brick and opened the rusty gate. The sound of the creaking iron shattered the silence and she suddenly realized that the wind had calmed. Dead leaves, still hanging from the trees, were now motionless.

She took a step forward. A twig snapped beneath her boot and she froze, her eyes on Tris. He paused for a moment, then turned around as if he sensed he was being followed. Hallie quickly stepped behind a massive oak beside the path and waited, her pulse pounding in her throat.

Could her aunts be right? Could Edward Tristan actually be a vampire come to search for her uncle Nicholas? All their warnings suddenly came rushing back to her mind, all the evidence they'd collected against him suddenly meshing with his odd behavior.

Hallie closed her eyes and shook her head. No! She didn't believe in the existence of vampires! Tris was probably a vampire hunter like all the other loonies in town.

She peered around the tree and noticed that Tris had unlocked the gate and disappeared inside. Darting for the shadows of the brick wall, she stumbled over a rotting log. She bit back a scream as she fell headfirst into a muddy patch on the path. But Hallie kept her wits about her and an instant later was back on her feet and headed for cover. A few moments more and she'd made her way to the gate. Pressing her body against the brick pillars that flanked the entrance to the cemetery, she looked inside. With silent footsteps, she made her way through the gate and hid behind a tall marker, squatting down to gain a perfect view of Tris.

He stood at the foot of her uncle's grave, staring down at the ground around his feet. He kicked at the leaves that covered the hard ground, then moved to study the headstone. Setting the lantern on the ground, he bent and looked at something at the base of the marker.

Hallie shivered and rubbed her icy hands together. "Come on," she muttered beneath her breath. "It's cold out here."

She stifled a groan as Tris sat down next to the grave and braced his arms on his knees. If she left now, he'd surely see her. But if she didn't leave, she'd probably freeze to death right on the spot. All she could hope for was that he might fall asleep and she would be able to sneak out without being detected.

But he didn't sleep. He just sat for what seemed like hours, until Hallie's toes and fingers were numb and she was sure hypothermia wasn't far behind. She considered revealing her presence, but decided to wait just a few minutes longer. Finally, he stood and strode out, closing the gate behind him.

Hallie counted to thirty before she tried to stand. Moaning, she straightened her stiff legs and stretched her sore back. Then she hobbled over to Uncle Nick's grave and turned on her flashlight, searching the ground for clues to Tris's purpose.

A glint caught the beam of light and she bent to scratch the leaves away. Lying on the withered grass was an ornate signet ring. She picked it up and studied it under the light. Her breath caught in her throat as she read the initials inscribed on the ring. "N.R.T.," she murmured, "Nicholas Redfield Tyler."

She frowned, examining the ring more closely. It looked clean and shiny, not at all tarnished from its time in the dirt and the rain. Had it been here for over seventy years or had it just been placed here? Her thoughts returned to Tris and his purpose this night. Had he placed the ring on the grave? And if he had, why?

Another shiver skittered along her spine. "What are you up to, Edward Tristan? And why do you spend so much time in this graveyard?" She tucked the ring inside her pocket, determined to get answers to all her questions.

She stood and hurried to the gate. Grabbing hold of the bars, she shoved her shoulder against the rusty iron, but it wouldn't budge. It was then that she realized that Tris had locked the gate behind him. And the key was now well beyond her reach.

Hallie groaned in frustration. "How am I supposed to get out of here?" she cried. Twisted vines covered the tall brick wall. She'd crawled in and out of the cemetery as a child, but she'd been a lot more nimble—and courageous—in her youth. Then again, she wasn't about to spend the night in a cemetery with a suspected vampire sleeping close by.

"Well, it's either scale the wall, or spend the night with Uncle Nick." With that, she pulled her nightgown between her legs and knotted it in front of her. "All of this for Edward Tristan," she muttered. "I should have turned him away that very first night!"

4

A BELL JINGLED above her head as Hallie pushed open the front door of the general store. She dug into her jacket pocket for her grocery list. Her hand closed around the ring she'd found in the cemetery a few nights ago.

She wasn't sure what to do about it. She'd considered confronting Tris and demanding to know whether he'd placed the ring on the grave himself, but she'd been deliberately avoiding him over the past few days. The aunts would have been no help. Discovery of the ring would only give them more to gossip about. Perhaps a search of the attic might provide an explanation for the ring's sudden appearance.

Hallie tucked the ring back into her pocket, then stepped inside the grocery store. The scarred plank floor creaked beneath her feet and the smell of fresh baked goods teased at her nose. Hester Cromwell, Abner's wife, glanced up from her newspaper spread on the counter, then tipped her chin up and squinted at Hallie through her reading glasses. "Afternoon, Hallie. Fine day out there, eh?"

Hallie nodded and grabbed a shopping basket from the end of the counter. "Good afternoon, Hester. How are you?"

Hester shifted on her stool and winced. "Good as can be expected. My bones ache with the damp, but you can't stop winter from comin' on. Almanac says it'll be a mild one though." She studied Hallie for a long moment. "What happened to you?"

Hallie's fingers touched her face and she forced a smile. "I had a little run-in with a branch. I was doing some gardening," she lied. In fact, her legs and arms looked much worse than her face. The vines on the cemetery wall had taken their toll on her. And she had a huge bruise on her backside from when she'd landed hard on the other side.

"Hear tell you have yourself a vampire stayin' up in your coach house," Hester commented.

Hallie froze, her hand resting on a can of tomato paste stacked high at the end of the first aisle. Hester Cromwell was usually a veritable fount of town gossip, but Hallie and her inn had rarely provided her with anything of interest. It had been Hallie's only goal in life to be so uninteresting that no one bothered to talk about her. She slowly turned to face the gray-haired woman's inquiring expression. "What was that?"

She nodded. "Ah-yup. The Sisters were in here 'round lunchtime. Couldn't stop talking about the man. Says he's holed up in your coach house. Doesn't eat, doesn't come out in the daytime. My Abner was right." She shook her finger to emphasize her claim to her husband's brilliance. "These vampire folks are going to put Egg Harbor on the map. And once they find out we got ourselves a real vampire, even more will come running."

Hallie shoved the tomato paste back onto the shelf and stepped over to the counter. "Hester, there are no such things as vampires," she insisted. "They don't exist. And the Sisters don't have a clue as to what they're talking about. Tris—I mean, Mr. Tristan—is not a vampire. He simply values his privacy, that's all. Now, I'd appreciate it if that rumor would stop right here. My guests should not be the subject of gossip."

"Maybe you don't believe in vampires," Hester countered, "but plenty of other folks do. And those folks have money." She grabbed a flyer from the counter and waved it beneath Hallie's nose. "Take a look. We're going to have ourselves a regular Vampire Festival. Folks will come from all over. Rockboro's been gloating over their Rutabaga Festival for years. All that hoop-dee-do over a vegetable nobody can stand to eat. Well, we'll show 'em just what a real festival is all about."

Hallie snatched the flyer from Hester's hand. She skimmed the text, her heart sinking with each word. "How could they do this?" she murmured. "Don't they realize what this will do to Egg Harbor?"

"The town board decided to strike while the iron was hot," Hester said. "They've been in meetings day and night to get this planned. There's goin' to be a parade. And the Sisters even offered to help. They're going to call that reporter they know at the *New York Times* and have him run an article on the festivities. And they'll be stagin' a play, too. Something by a French guy. Auditions are tomorrow night at the town hall."

"Prudence and Patience have offered to help with the festival?"

"Ah-yup. They got to talking with Abner and they're real excited. After all, the Tylers have vampires hangin' in the family tree. Who better to get involved but the Sisters?" Hester frowned. "Can't for the life of me figure out the pumpkins, though."

"Pumpkins?" Hallie asked.

"Yeah. The Sisters came in here looking for watermelons. We haven't had watermelons for months. Then they said they'd take all the pumpkins I had. Cleaned me right out. You plannin' to make a bunch of pies? I told them canned pumpkin was easier, but once somethin' gets set in their heads, there's no knockin' it loose. Just wouldn't hear of it, I tell you."

Hallie tucked her grocery list back into her pocket. "That's not all they haven't been hearing lately." She yanked the door open and the bell jangled furiously.

"Where ya goin'?" Hester called.

"To shake some sense into two crazy old women," Hallie muttered, slamming the door behind her.

Hallie headed for her Jeep parked in front of the store, but a familiar figure waved to her from the other side of the street. "Miss Tyler! Miss Tyler! It's me, Newton Knoblock. Good day, Miss Tyler."

Hallie groaned and pasted a bright smile onto her face as she watched the tweed-clad man dodge a pickup truck. Breathlessly, he stopped in front of her and pulled a handkerchief from his pocket and blew his nose. Poor Newton seemed to have perpetual postnasal drip. He had already sniffled his way through two boxes of tissues since his arrival at the Widow's Walk. He'd come with three other vampire hunters from East Orange, New Jersey.

"We found some clues in the graveyard last night," he said. "The grave had been disturbed. I believe your uncle Nicholas will make an appearance soon."

"That's nice, Mr. Knoblock."

He sniffled and gave her a moony-eyed look. "You can call me Newton," he said. "After all, I've been staying at your inn for over a week now. We should become better friends, don't you think?"

"I don't think we have much in common, Mr. Knoblock. After all, I don't believe in vampires and you do. What would we ever find to talk about?"

She didn't wait for him to reply, but jumped into her Jeep and made a quick U-turn on Main Street, leaving Newton standing forlornly on the sidewalk, before speeding back up the road toward the inn.

As if Prudence and Patience weren't enough of a problem, now she had Newton Knoblock to deal with. She felt as if she was the only one in Egg Harbor with a grip on reality. All twelve of her guests spent most of their waking hours waiting for her uncle Nicholas to pop out of his grave. Things had gotten so bad she was considering erecting bleachers around the family plot and charging admission.

The townsfolk cared only for the money to be made from the undead. And Prudence and Patience had managed to start the whole thing with their misguided efforts at marketing. And then there was the mystifying Edward Tristan.

To bring one of her guests into the mess was unforgivable! Tris was not a vampire! He was simply a man—an attractive, compelling, incredibly sexy man. And a man she couldn't seem to resist, no matter how hard she tried.

Her thoughts drifted back to the kiss they'd shared and her fingers came up to touch her lips. At first she'd thought it was just a dream, another hazy journey into a fantasy that would never be fulfilled. But then he'd spoken and she had realized she wasn't dreaming. Edward Tristan had kissed her! And she hadn't done anything to stop him.

Why couldn't she resist him? And why did he seem to be a constant presence in her thoughts, waking and sleeping? It was as if he held some unnatural power over her, arousing passions and desires she never knew she possessed. Yes, she still wanted him to kiss her! The truth be told, she wouldn't have stopped him if he'd tossed her over his shoulder and carried her off to the bedroom.

Hallie scolded herself silently. Just a few nights ago at the graveyard she'd decided that Edward Tristan might just be a vampire. Yet, even considering that notion, she was still fantasizing about the man! He couldn't be a vampire, she repeated to herself.

So what if he liked to visit graveyards? There had to be a logical reason for his nighttime wanderings. Perhaps he was an insomniac and a brisk walk relaxed him. And he had told her that he had a keen interest in the local history.

Hallie groaned and pushed all thoughts of Edward Tristan to the back of her mind as she turned up the drive to the inn. She stopped the Jeep with a skid and jumped out, then hurried toward the front door. She found Prudence and Patience standing on the porch, dressed in identical camel hair coats, their handbags dangling from their arms and a couple dozen pumpkins at their feet. Patience bent down and hefted one into her arms.

"Don't drop it, Sister!" Prudence cried. "If you drop it, it might not work."

"I'm not going to drop it, Sister," Patience countered. "I told you we should have had Hester deliver these. Fifty dollars' worth of pumpkins should warrant free delivery, don't you think? Now, open the front door for me."

Hallie crossed her arms over her chest and watched them. "What is going on here?"

They both turned to her and smiled in relief. "Thank goodness you're here, dear," Prudence said. "Look at this mess. It took us an hour to carry them up the steps from the car. And they nearly filled the trunk of the Packard. Come and help us, Hallie. We have to hurry and get these inside or it might not work. As it is, it rarely works outside of Romania."

"What might not work?" Hallie asked, taking the steps two at a time. She grabbed the pumpkin from Patience.

"They might not turn into vampires," Prudence replied as if her words made all the sense in the world.

Hallie placed the pumpkin at her feet and straightened, her hands braced on her hips. "Vampires?"

"It's an old Gypsy legend," Patience began in earnest.

"From the Balkans," Prudence continued. "The transformation is supposed to happen with watermelons, too, but we had trouble finding watermelons this time of year."

"If you keep a pumpkin inside for more than ten days," Patience explained, "it may turn into a vampire. Sister recalled reading this in a book and we decided to give it a try. The Vampire Festival is less than three weeks away and if all these pumpkins work, we could have a whole chorus of vampires among us."

Hallie shook her head in exasperation. "You expect these pumpkins to magically turn into vampires?"

"Not instantly. It takes time," Patience said. "Ten days. Or one can keep them after Christmas, but we can't wait that long. They're supposed to start rolling around the floor and growling first. That's how you know they're about to turn. And then there's the drop of blood. We're going to put these all in the parlor. With people coming and going, we should be able to keep an eye on them."

"Sister, do you think they'll appear fully clothed?" Prudence mused. "Or will they be . . ." Two spots of color rose in her cheeks and she placed her fingers over her lips. "Naked," she whispered, wincing at the word.

Prudence frowned, considering her sister's question. "I'm not sure, Sister. But I suppose it would be best to be prepared. We should have appropriate clothes at the ready."

"The only thing that's going to happen in ten days," Hallie interrupted, "is that I'm going to have two dozen rotten pumpkins stinking up my parlor. You will not bring those inside."

"Perhaps we could keep them in our room?" Patience offered.

"We'd promise to watch them," Prudence said. "And they won't disturb the guests. We'll try to keep the growling and the rolling to a minimum."

"They won't make noise because they're pumpkins!" Hallie said, her voice rising in volume with each word. "Big orange vegetables, nothing more. We eat them in pie and carve them up on Halloween and sometimes we toast the seeds. But beyond that, there's not much use for them except as oversize doorstops."

"Then you won't let us bring them inside?" Prudence asked.

"If you want to carry them up to your room, feel free. But I'm not going to help you. And you'll just have to carry them back down again when they get all slimy and start to smell bad."

"We can do that," they both said.

"And another thing," Hallie continued. "I'd appreciate it if you would put an end to all this ridiculous speculation about Mr. Tristan. He is a paying guest at the Widow's Walk and not to be made the subject of town gossip." She opened the front door. "What were you two thinking?"

The Sisters tagged along behind her, leaving their legion of pumpkin vampires on the porch. "You shouldn't be so close-minded, dear," Patience said. "We have evidence. It's not a rumor if one has solid evidence. Besides, passing gossip would be unseemly. Mother taught us that!"

"You have no evidence," Hallie said, "except what's rattling around in your two very overactive imaginations."

"That's not so," Prudence admonished. "The man is never seen in sunlight. All day long the Do Not Disturb sign hangs from his door. No matter how much food we bring him, he won't eat a bite. And we went to make up the bed with fresh linens . . ." She paused for dramatic effect. "It hasn't been slept in."

"And he leaves at all hours of the night. Sister and I have seen him walking down toward the graveyard the past two nights. We've been watching from our window."

Hallie swallowed hard. So she wasn't the only person to witness Mr. Tristan's nighttime habits. "You've been spying on Mr. Tristan?"

"We haven't been spying. We've been making careful note of his nocturnal behavior. It's a sign, you know. Sister found a book about it."

"All the signs are there."

"Of course, he doesn't have the hairy palms," Patience added. "And we haven't gotten a good look at his teeth. The teeth would be the real clue."

"And there is the reluctance to enter a house without an invitation," Prudence said.

Hallie's mind flashed back to the night Tris had first appeared in the doorway of the inn. He had stood there for a long time before stepping inside. In fact, he'd waited for her invitation. And he was a bit pale. And then there was the rather unusual effect he had on her resolve. And his strange trip to the graveyard.

She cursed silently. Was she losing her mind? She didn't believe a word of this malarkey her aunts were spouting. "You two will stay away from Mr. Tristan, do you understand? From now on, I'll take care of his meals and his room."

They both nodded. "That would probably be best, dear. We're bound to be busy with the play."

"The play?"

"Sister and I have been chosen to coordinate the artistic contribution to the First Annual Egg Harbor Vampire Festival. We're staging a community production of a scene from Mr. Alexandre Dumas's play of 1851, called *The Vampire*. It will be the grand finale of the entire weekend. An event not to be missed. Of course, since you're related to the producers, we'll make sure there's a part in it for you, Hallie. There is a virgin in this play, isn't there, Sister?"

Hallie opened her mouth to correct Prudence's assumption, but decided her sex life was not a fit subject for this discussion. The reality of her sexual experience was not that earth-shattering, but it was enough to give her maiden aunts the vapors. Besides, if her status as a virgin hadn't been reinstated after so many celibate years in Egg Harbor, it surely should have been.

"And we plan to hold some of our rehearsals and production meetings here at the inn. You don't mind, do you, dear? Our dining room is so spacious. The town hall just has that old potbelly stove to heat it and it's quite chilly in the evenings."

Hallie sighed. "You can hold your rehearsals here under one condition."

"What is that, dear?" they asked in tandem.

"You will not spread any more gossip about Mr. Tristan. And you'll keep the rest of your vampire fantasies to yourselves—including Uncle Nicholas. I don't want to hear another word about vampires beneath this roof, do you understand?"

"But what about the play? It will be hard to rehearse a play called *The Vampire* without saying 'vampire', don't you think? And we've planned a meeting for tonight to discuss the auditions."

Hallie groaned and started for the linen room. "Just don't mention that word around me or you and your troupe will be freezing your backsides off at the town hall. Now, if you two will excuse me, I'm going to make up Mr. Tristan's room."

"But the sun hasn't set," Prudence warned. "And the sign will be on the door."

Hallie waved her hand over her head dismissively as she shoved the kitchen door open. It was about time she got to the bottom of Edward Tristan's behavior! If she wanted to know if he was a vampire, she'd simply ask him.

TRIS BRACED his hands on the wall of the shower stall and bent his head, letting the hot water sluice down his back. He had slept most of the day away, drifting off on the sofa, as he had every other morning, his computer flickering on the coffee table.

For the first time in a very long time, he actually believed he might finish this book. The first draft was going exceedingly well and he'd already decided to stay in Egg Harbor until it was finished.

Tris turned off the water and stepped out of the shower stall. After he quickly toweled off, he tugged on his jeans, leaving the top button open, then padded out to the great room in search of his glasses. He stopped when he caught sight of the antique cuff link he'd placed on the coffee table. Picking it up, he studied it beneath the lamp.

He'd found the piece a few nights ago in the graveyard, tossed on top of the dead grass and leaves. He frowned. Someone had gone to plenty of trouble to plant clues near Nicholas Tyler's grave. But who?

There were plenty of townsfolk who had a vested interest in perpetuating the hoax. And then there were all the vampire hunters in town. Last but not least, there was Hallie Tyler herself. But considering Hallie's opinion of the matter, he could safely rule her out. Then, there was always the possibility of a real vampire.

Tris smiled to himself. He no more believed in the existence of vampires than Hallie did. Tris stared at the cuff link for a long moment, then placed it back on the table. If he hoped to please Hallie by proving the vampire legend a hoax, he'd have to do it after he finished his manuscript.

Running his fingers through his damp hair, Tris glanced out the window. The last sliver of sunshine had disappeared on the western horizon, marking the beginning of his workday. He pulled the drapes open, then walked to the door and opened it to remove the Do Not Disturb sign. He'd barely settled on the sofa when a sharp rap at the door disturbed the silence of the coach house.

Tris groaned. Who would it be tonight? Prudence or Patience? God forbid, both of them were on the other side of the door. As soon as the sun went down, they seemed to appear with one excuse after another to bother him. And they made themselves very difficult to get rid of.

He walked back to the door and pulled it open. But to his delight Hallie stood on the other side, a stack of towels and sheets tucked beneath her arm. He smiled and leaned against the edge of the door. "Hello, Hallie."

"Hello, Mr— Hello, Tris." She stared at him nervously. "I brought . . . fresh towels," she murmured absently. "I would have come sooner, but the sign was on the door and I thought you were . . . asleep."

"Well, I'm not." He stepped aside. "Why don't you come in? I could use some company right about now."

Hesitantly, Hallie stepped past him into the coach house. "I'll just put these in the bathroom. I've brought linens for the bed, as well. My aunts said they hadn't been able to get in and make it up for the past few days." She hurried toward the bedroom, then stopped short at the door. Since Tris hadn't slept in the bed since he'd arrived, the bed was perfectly made.

He stepped up behind her and bent close to her hair, taking a deep breath of the sweet smell. "I haven't been sleeping in the bed," he said, his gaze drifting along the nape of her neck.

She turned, as if surprised to find him standing so near. Lord, she was beautiful. He felt himself sway toward her, as if drawn by an undeniable force.

"Where have you been—" she swallowed hard "—sleeping?"

He shrugged as he took in the exquisite details of her face. "Here and there."

"You look tired."

He shook his head. "Not anymore. I just got up. I'm glad you're here. I'm famished."

Her eyes went wide. "You're hungry? The Sisters told me you haven't been eating."

"I find plenty to keep me alive," he said. He fought the temptation to reach out and touch her, to repeat the events of that night in the parlor. Tonight, she seemed distant, less approachable.

"You don't eat, you don't sleep. That doesn't sound like a very healthy life-style to me."

"I sleep," he said. "During the day. I'm just a night person. And I eat when I'm hungry."

Hallie swallowed hard. "A night person? Does that mean—" She stopped herself for a moment, then busied herself with straightening the edges of the clean linens she held. "You don't—like daylight."

"I know it's a bit unusual, but I've just adjusted to this kind of schedule. I'm much more comfortable in the dark. I hope that's not a problem for you."

"Problem? Oh, no! Not at all. No problem. Who am I to comment on your habits?"

He sensed her uneasiness and reached out to touch her arm, but she deftly evaded his touch and stepped around him to place the linens on the coffee table. He cleared his throat. "I meant that I hoped it wasn't a problem with making up the room. If you'd like to come later in the evening, that would be fine with me. Or simply leave the linens."

They stood silently for a long moment, staring at each other from across the room. Suddenly he felt as if all that had passed between them had never happened. She was acting like he was a complete stranger; not at all like the woman he'd held in his arms only a few nights before.

"I—I should really go," she murmured.

"No," Tris said softly. "Stay. Sit down." He crossed the room and took her arm, then led her to the couch.

She slowly sat down. "I—I hope you've enjoyed your stay."

He nodded then glanced around at his surroundings. "I like this place. It would make a nice home." He paused, then sank into the cushions of the sofa next to her. "When I was a little boy, my parents moved around a lot. Strange places, strange houses. Nothing really seemed like home."

"That must have been difficult for you," Hallie said.

"The first night in a new house, I used to stay up all night long waiting for the monsters under my bed to appear. I guess I learned to like the dark."

"Most children find it frightening," Hallie commented.

"It's not nearly as frightening as moving into a new town and finding new friends." He smiled ruefully. "When I was especially lonely, I used to make up scary stories. I'd try as hard as I could to frighten myself and then all the really scary things in my life didn't seem so bad. Sounds kind of demented, doesn't it?"

Hallie shook her head. "Not really. It explains a lot."

"About what?"

"About your need for privacy. Some people just like to be alone. I can understand that."

He grabbed her hand and looked into her eyes. "I don't always want to be alone," he said, toying with her delicate fingers.

"No," she murmured, her cheeks flushing.

"Hallie, what's wrong? Did I frighten you when I kissed you the other night?"

She averted her gaze and shook her head. "You surprised me, that's all."

"And would you like me to kiss you now?"

She shook her head more emphatically and stood. "I think it would be best if you didn't. It would be wrong for me to get . . . involved with a guest."

"And why is that?" Tris asked.

"Because guests always go home," she said. "And you're supposed to leave tomorrow."

With that, she turned and hurried to the door, leaving Tris to watch her retreat. The door slammed behind her with a startling finality and Tris sighed and sank back into the soft cushions of the sofa. He shook his head and frowned.

If he'd thought he was making progress with Hallie Tyler, he'd been deluding himself. She'd run out of the coach house as if he'd posed a threat to her safety. What could have possibly put that idea into her head?

"WHAT DO YOU SUPPOSE it is?" Prudence asked, her eyes wide.

Patience cocked her head and stared at the crate from her place on the front porch. "It looks to be about the size of a coffin, Sister," she replied in a loud whisper.

Hallie turned and shushed her aunt from the bottom of the steps. "Don't be ridiculous. It's not a coffin." She turned her attention back to the delivery man who was wrestling the seven-foot-tall crate up onto a handcart. "What's in the crate, if I might ask?"

The grizzled trucker squinted down at his clipboard. His brows shot up. "A coffin," he replied. "Somebody die?"

Hallie gulped hard and blinked back her surprise. "You're joking," she said.

"Says here, I'm supposed to deliver this directly to a Mr. Edward Tristan right after sunset and not a minute before." He looked up at the sky, then down at his watch. "That would be about now, I'd reckon. Where should I put it?"

"I don't understand," Hallie said. "Why would Mr. Tristan order a coffin?"

A duet of clucking tongues sounded from behind her and she glanced at her aunts, giving them a warning glare. In return, they sent her an I-told-you-so look.

The trucker flipped through the pages on his clipboard. "He didn't order it," the man said. "It was ordered by someone named L. Darman from New York City."

"Who is that?"

The trucker gave her an impatient look. "I don't know. Maybe it's his undertaker. Listen, lady, I've got a load of rocking chairs I have to deliver to Bangor before nine tonight. Can we quit with the questions and get this thing delivered? Where do I find this Mr. Tristan?"

"I'll show you the way!" Prudence cried.

"And I'll help!" Patience added.

At that moment, Newton Knoblock pushed between the aunts and peered through his bottle-bottomed glasses at the activity taking place in the driveway. He dabbed at his nose with the ever-present handkerchief and straightened his bow tie. "Is that a coffin?" he asked in his nasal whine, a sound grating enough to make the aunts wince and step away. "It looks like a coffin. Why would you be ordering a coffin, Miss Tyler? Are you hiding something? Has Nicholas Tyler reappeared?"

Hallie ground her teeth and held out her hand to silence the truck driver. "No, Mr. Knoblock, I'm not hiding anything. And this isn't a coffin. It's—a new linen chest for the upstairs hallway."

"It sure looks like a coffin to me," he said.

"Mr. Knoblock, I believe your little group has already left for the graveyard. If you don't hurry you might miss something . . . like a vampire or two."

He stumbled down the front steps and gave the crate a suspicious look, then gazed at Hallie adoringly. "The blueberry muffins were a little dry this morning, but I liked them. I just thought you'd like to know. And the restaurant you recommended for dinner didn't have liver on the menu. It's important to have a daily source of iron, you know. And I thought I told you to call me Newton."

Hallie forced a smile. "I appreciate your comments, Newton. Now, you'd better hurry along. I wouldn't want you to miss anything."

She watched as Newton rushed down the drive to the main road. Sighing, she turned her gaze to her aunts. "And you'll both stay right where you are," she said. "I'll show this man where to put the cof—crate." She motioned to the driver and he tipped the crate back on the handcart and followed her. The going got rough as the path to the coach house narrowed, and Hallie had to guide him slowly to the front door. This time, no sign hung from the knob. She rapped sharply and within moments Tris appeared.

He brushed his long hair back from his eyes and stared down at her through wire-rimmed glasses. This time, unlike the last, he had all his clothes on. He was dressed entirely in black, his turtleneck emphasizing his broad shoulders and narrow waist. "Hallie! I was just thinking about you. Come on in."

She shifted uneasily and stepped aside. "You . . . you have a delivery," she murmured. "And I have to get back to the house."

"Wait," he said, reaching out to grab her arm. "You can stay for a while. Come on." Almost against her will, he pulled her inside. She tried to resist him, but it was as if he had trapped her in his spell again. He caught sight of the driver behind her and raised a brow. "Can I help you?"

"You Mr. Edward Tristan?" the driver asked.

Tris nodded and the driver shoved the clipboard at him. "Sign here," he said.

Tris glanced at the crate. "What is it?"

The driver maneuvered the crate inside the door and rolled it into the center of the room, then slipped it off the handcart. "Ask the lady, mister. I'm through answering questions." He pulled the door shut behind him, leaving Hallie and Tris alone in the silent coach house.

"Why don't you open it?" Hallie said softly, her voice holding a hint of challenge.

Tris stepped up to the crate and ran his hand along the edge. "It's nailed shut."

"I'll get some tools." Hallie hurried to the spare bedroom where she stored her tools and came back with a hammer and a crowbar. Tristan studied the crate for a moment, then grabbed the top end and lowered it onto the hardwood floor.

"It's from an L. Darman," Hallie said as he worked at the rough pine boards with the tools.

Tristan chuckled. "Louise," he murmured. "This should be good."

The cover of the crate popped off and Tris yanked back a sheet of cardboard to reveal a gleaming mahogany— Hallie drew a deep breath. "It's a coffin," she said softly.

"Yup," Tris said, grinning. "That's about it." He reached inside the crate and pulled the coffin open. "Satin-lined. Looks pretty comfy, don't you think?" He turned to Hallie, humor lighting his normally serious expression. He tore the rest of the crate apart until the coffin stood on the floor in all its gleaming glory. He ran his hand along the smooth wood. "Very nice. Kind of classy, don't you think?"

Hallie rocked nervously on her heels, then watched in horror as he stepped inside the coffin and laid down, crossing his hands over his chest.

"Close the lid," he said.

She gasped. "What?" Hallie stepped back and shook her head. "No!"

"Come on, Hallie. I want to see what it feels like. Just for a minute, okay?"

Hallie headed for the door. "Absolutely not! I'll clean your room, I'll bring you your meals, but I will not—tuck you in for the night—or the day—or whatever!"

Tris jumped out of the coffin and followed her. "Hallie, it's only a coffin. Where's your sense of humor?"

She bristled and crossed her arms beneath her breasts, then turned to face him. This had gone way too far! "You're a guest here. And your personal habits are none of my business. If you choose to sleep in a coffin or pursue an . . ." She took a deep breath. "Alternative life-style, then that's your business. And none of mine."

She opened her mouth, ready to make the accusation that she hadn't had the courage to spit out the last time she visited the coach house. But suddenly the prospect of saying the word "vampire" seemed laughingly ridiculous. Coffin or not, the man standing in front of her was as warm-blooded as she was. "I have to go," she murmured. "I'm very busy."

She hurried to the door, giving the coffin one last look as she passed. The sooner she got rid of Edward Tristan, the sooner she could regain her sanity. Pausing at the door, she turned back to him. "You're scheduled to check out tomorrow morning before noon. Just call the house and let me know when you'd like your final bill prepared."

"I'm not leaving," Tris said.

Hallie's breath caught in her throat. "What?"

He raised an eyebrow. "I said, I'm not leaving. I've decided to extend my stay. At least until the end of the month. Perhaps indefinitely. Is that a problem?"

She swallowed hard. "No! I—I mean, yes."

"Well, what is it? No or yes?"

Hallie felt her cheeks warm beneath his gaze. "No," she said softly, knowing that to refuse the business now would be foolish. "No problem at all." With that, she turned and strode out of the coach house. Halfway down the path, she stopped and turned back. But after a few steps she changed her mind.

What did she care whether Edward Tristan was alive or undead? Or whether he stayed until Christmas? From now on, she was going to give the man a wide berth. And she was going to leave the clean towels and sheets at the front door.

5

TRIS PULLED the front door of the coach house shut behind him just as the sun's rays disappeared in the west. The weather had turned unusually warm for mid-October, a balmy breeze blowing off the bluff and skittering across the glassy surface of the Atlantic.

He'd been working almost nonstop for the past three days but had finally decided to get some sleep. From six that morning until six that night, he had slept—twelve hours of glorious, dreamless sleep. Reaching above his head, he stretched and tried to work the kinks out of his neck. Well-rested and ravenous, he felt like a bear just out of hibernation. Right now, he needed a big meal and a healthy dose of Hallie Tyler. The isolation and too many take-out meals from Earl's had begun to wear thin.

He hadn't seen Hallie since she'd helped deliver the coffin from Louise. Leave it to Louise to send him such an outrageous gift. He probably shouldn't have called his agent and told her about his new vampire plot. But she'd been in almost constant contact with his publisher and they both needed to know that the new book was going well. They also needed to know that he'd be staying in Egg Harbor a little longer. What they didn't need to know about was the upcoming Egg Harbor Vampire Festival.

He'd casually mentioned the craziness that had descended on this quiet seacoast town, the events of each day recounted by Earl during Tris's late night visits to the diner. Louise couldn't have been more excited if he'd just told her he'd just won the Pulitzer.

The truth be told, he should have thought of it earlier, but Tris had never been interested in promoting himself or his work. He left that in the very capable hands of his publicist, a publicist who considered Tris a very reluctant subject at best. The combination of a real vampire legend, a small-town festival and the upcoming release of his newest work was just the kind of hook George Kincaid dreamed about.

By the time he'd hung up the phone, he'd managed to convince Louise that he would call George immediately and give him what he needed to jumpstart the publicity plans for *Wicked Ways*. But Tris never made the call. He wasn't about to put his anonymity at risk with some splashy news story.

He needed more quiet time here to finish his book, but more importantly, he needed more time with Hallie Tyler—before he told her about Tristan Montgomery. After their last encounter, he wasn't quite sure where he stood with her. What seemed like an intense attraction had taken a sudden turn in the opposite direction. Well, he was about to put everything right back on track. He'd make her admit that there was something between them—or make a fool of himself trying.

Tris headed for the inn, whistling a soft tune as he walked. Perhaps he'd ask her to dinner. Or maybe they'd take a walk around the village. Or they could share a drink at a local watering hole. He didn't care what they did, just as long as they spent the next few hours together. But as he came around the corner of the house, he found Hallie well occupied with another task—and another man.

Tris stepped back into the shadows of the shrubbery and watched them both. Hallie was dressed in worn blue jeans, a figure-hugging T-shirt and muddy boots. His gaze skimmed the length of her slender body, lingering over the soft swell of her breasts and the gentle curve of her hips. His fingers clenched instinctively as he remembered what she felt like beneath his hands.

She worked feverishly with a rake, piling leaves and debris in neat piles that dotted the sweeping lawn. Her companion, dressed in a tweed sport jacket and bow tie, worked beside her, chattering as he clumsily stuffed leaves into large trash bags.

An unbidden flood of jealousy surged through Tris at the cozy domestic scene. Hallie's companion seemed incredibly attentive, following her around the lawn like a panting puppy, dragging a trash bag nearly as big as he was. Every now and then she'd give him a sideways glance and a coy smile, increasing Tris's jealousy a few degrees more.

She had turned that smile on him any number of times and he knew the astounding effect it could have a man, the addictive nature of such a simple expression and the desire it kindled. But he wasn't about to let this guy go up in flames as he had. Tris stepped out of the shadows and walked nonchalantly into the middle of the scene, determined to find out just where this man fit into Hallie's life.

"It would be better to chop these leaves and use them as mulch," the man commented as Tris approached. "More environmentally sound. Do you plan to cover those roses? It's best to cover roses in this climate, you know. I could cover those roses for you. Would you like that?"

Hallie turned to speak to the man, then caught sight of Tris's approach. A smile that looked like it was tinged with relief curled the corners of her mouth. "Mr. Tristan!"

The man spun around and stared at Tris from behind thick lenses. He withdrew a handkerchief from his pocket and blew his nose. "You're Mr. Tristan?" he asked, eyes wide, nose sniffling.

Tris frowned and gave Hallie a questioning look. "Yes, I am," he said hesitantly.

The man peered up at him, examining Tris as if he were some strange new germ under a microscope. "I've heard about you," he said warily.

"Mr. Tristan, this is Mr. Knoblock. He's a guest here at the inn. He's interested in vampires."

"Newton Knoblock," he said, holding out his hand. "President of the East Orange chapter of Undead International. We're an organization devoted to the discovery, appreciation and proliferation of vampires throughout the world."

Tris didn't return his handshake, but simply smiled at the strange little man and gave him a curt nod. "Mr. Knoblock."

Newton frowned and stared at Tris more intently. "Have we met?" he asked. "Your face looks familiar to me. I never forget a face. I was just telling Hallie that very thing. I never forget a face."

Tris turned away and looked out across the bluff at the ocean beyond. Considering Newton's interest in the supernatural, chances were the man had read at least one of Tristan Montgomery's books. Tris weighed his chances of escape before detection, but then decided speaking with Hallie was well worth the risk. Besides, Newton Knoblock didn't seem too quick off the mark. And from the other side of those thick lenses, there was no telling what Tris looked like.

"If you'll excuse me, Mr. Knoblock, I'd like to speak with Miss Tyler privately for a moment. There's a problem with my room." Tris stepped by the man, grabbed Hallie's arm, and pulled her along with him until they'd rounded the corner of the house.

Hallie sighed as she pulled off her leather work gloves, then peeked back at Newton. "Thank you for rescuing me."

"I didn't realize you needed rescuing," Tris replied softly, taking in the fresh features of her face, her rosy cheeks and the brilliant green of her eyes.

Hallie smiled winsomely, sending a frisson of desire shooting through Tristan's body. "Newton is here looking for my uncle Nicholas. He thinks if he sticks close by me he'll catch me slipping Uncle Nick table scraps."

"I think he's hanging around you for entirely different reasons," Tris commented. "The man is besotted."

Hallie met his gaze. "What do you mean?"

"I think he has a personal interest in you."

She stared down at her gloves, picking at a spot of dirt on one of the palms. "What makes you think that?"

Tris reached out and ran his finger down her bare arm. "Let's just say I'm familiar with the symptoms. Come on, Hallie, you have to know how incredibly attractive men find you."

Hallie took a long breath. "Listen, Mr. Tristan, I—"

"It's Tris," he interrupted. "And if you're going to give me that line about not mixing with the guests, I don't want to hear it."

"Even if it's the truth?" Hallie countered.

He grabbed Hallie by the arms and pulled her against him, then brought his mouth down on hers. For a moment she stiffened against him, but as his lips moved against hers, he felt her grow pliant in his arms. "It's not the truth," he murmured against her mouth. "And you know it."

"No," she said breathlessly, looking up at him with wide eyes. "Maybe not."

He grinned. "Why are you trying so hard to ignore what's happening between us? Why do you refuse to acknowledge it?"

She turned away from him, a look of dismay etched on her perfect features. "I don't know what you mean. Nothing is happening between us."

"Then you aren't attracted to me?" he asked. "And you'd rather I just stay away from you?"

"Yes," she murmured.

He shook his head. Lord, the woman could be stubborn! How could she ignore what she felt when he kissed her, the way she warmed to his touch? "I could stay away from you, Hallie, but you can't stay away from me."

She gasped and her gaze snapped back to his, her eyes filled with indignation at his statement. "Of all the egotistical, arrogant—"

He placed his finger over her lips to stop her outburst. "Admit it. No matter how hard you try, you're drawn to me."

"I am not!" she cried.

He chuckled, then tipped her chin up until she looked directly into his gaze. "Are you sure about that? Tell me you don't dream about us at night. Tell me you aren't tempted by my touch. Tell me you'd rather that I never kissed you again."

"All right," she said, her voice filled with defensiveness. "You want it, here it is. I don't dream about us, I'd prefer you kept your hands to yourself, and I'd rather kiss a dead codfish than be kissed by you."

Tris pulled her closer and brushed his lips against hers. "I don't believe you," he murmured. "And I daresay I'm a much better kisser than some old fish and you know it."

Suddenly he let go of her and she stumbled back, her knees buckling slightly. He smiled in satisfaction, her wobbly legs proving his point. But she recovered quickly and an instant later stood steely spined in front of him, her face flushed with anger. "Stay away from me, Mr. Tristan," she warned.

"Is that a challenge?" he asked. "Because if it is, I dare *you* to stay away from *me*. I don't think you can."

She gave him a haughty look, then a smug smile. "I guess we'll just have to see, won't we."

Tris shrugged. "I guess."

With that, she turned on her heel and walked directly into the shrubbery. She cursed softly as she flailed for her balance, then turned again and managed to navigate the corner of the house. Tris watched her leave, shook his head and chuckled. For him to raise such high emotion in Hallie Tyler had to mean something. And he was nearly certain that it meant things between them were exactly as he suspected.

Hallie was as attracted to him as he was to her. She just wasn't ready to admit it. But he had time to wait. And he suspected that Hallie would be well worth waiting for.

HALLIE PULLED OFF her gardening gloves and threw them on the table beside the front door, then tugged off her muddy boots. As she wrestled the last one off, she hopped backward across the hardwood floor. Cursing, she gave the boot one last angry tug, which sent her skidding backwards on the polished floor until she landed on her backside with a thud.

She heaped a few more colorful epithets on Edward Tristan's character and his considerable ego before she groaned and laid back on the floor. She stared up at the ceiling. "He doesn't think I can stay away from him? Who the hell does he think he is?"

"Miss Tyler? Are you all right?"

Hallie pushed up on her elbows only to find Newton Knoblock staring at her from beyond the sofa. He shoved his glasses up onto his nose and sniffled, clutching a book to his chest. Hallie felt her cheeks warm with embarrassment as she crawled to her feet. "I'm fine, Mr. Knoblock."

"Newton," he said.

"Newton," Hallie repeated. "I thought you'd be off with your group by now."

"I decided to stay and do some reading. Our yard work rather exhausted me. And I wanted to talk to you about this Mr. Tristan."

Hallie held up her hand and shook her head. "I don't want to hear anything more about Mr. Tristan. I've heard quite enough."

Newton hurried out from behind the sofa, tripping on the rug as he approached. He steadied himself and took a deep breath. "There's something about him I don't like. I think you should stay as far away from him as possible. I think he might be . . ."

Hallie waited for the word, knowing exactly what was coming. Obviously her aunts had been filling Newton's ear with their vampire gossip. And Newton had probably told his whole group by now.

"Dangerous," Newton said.

"Dangerous?"

"I daresay a man like that would never appreciate a woman like you. A woman of such gentle breeding and tender sensibilities. He would take you and use you, then discard you like yesterday's newspaper."

Hallie struggled to her feet, then patted Newton on the shoulder. "You don't have to worry about me, Mr. Knoblock. I can take care of myself."

"But you may not be able to resist," Newton said. "A man like Mr. Tristan has powerful forces at his disposal."

She studied him shrewdly. "Have you been talking to my aunts about Mr. Tristan?"

Newton shifted nervously on his feet. "They told me not to say anything to you. I'm afraid I've broken their confidence. But for good reason. I'm only trying to protect you. I've come to care for you, Miss Tyler."

Hallie picked up her boots and arranged them on the mat beside the door. "So you think Mr. Tristan is a vampire?" she asked, trying to sound indifferent.

Newton screwed up his face and he pondered the question. "I'm not entirely convinced," he said. "My instincts tell me no. But vampires are a very clever breed. They rely on subterfuge to survive in our world. I could be wrong about Mr. Tristan and you could be in grave danger. He seems to be very attracted to you. And virgins do hold a particular fascination for vampires."

Hallie bit her bottom lip to keep from laughing out loud. First her aunts and now Mr. Knoblock. Was it the way she acted? Or had a big *V* been tattooed on her forehead when she wasn't looking? Why did everyone assume she was a virgin? Sure, it had been a long time since she'd been to bed with a man, but she certainly hadn't imagined the whole experience! "I don't think we have to worry about Mr. Tristan on that count," Hallie said.

"No, we don't," Newton replied, puffing out his chest. "Because I'm here to protect you. I'll stay with you night and day. I won't let any harm come to you."

"That's really not necessary, Mr. Knoblock."

"Oh, but it is," he replied in earnest. "And it's no bother. I like spending time with you, Hallie."

Hallie forced a weak smile. "But you have so many other commitments. What about your group and your search for my uncle Nicholas? I'm sure he's out there waiting for you, somewhere. Perhaps you could just tell me what to watch out for. And if I see anything suspicious, I promise to come right to you."

He shook his head in adamant refusal. "I'm afraid it might already be too late by that time. I couldn't let you take that risk."

"All right," Hallie said. "Just suppose that we did have a vampire in our midst. How would I get rid of him?"

Newton's eyes lit up. "You want my advice?" he asked in a breathless voice.

Hallie nodded, then walked over to the registration desk to check for her messages. Newton followed on her heels.

"There are many different ways," he began. "You could decapitate the vampire with a shovel belonging to either a gravedigger or a sexton."

Hallie winced at the image. Though she might find a certain satisfaction in giving Tris a good whack with a shovel, she certainly didn't want to decapitate him. "I'm afraid that won't work," Hallie said. "My shovel came from the hardware store in Bangor. And I don't think we have a single gravedigger or sexton here in Egg Harbor."

"Well, you could use your shovel to drive an aspen stake through his heart," Newton suggested. "Of course, I'd be happy to do that for you. A woman as delicate as you probably wouldn't have the strength."

Hallie shook her head. "That option really doesn't appeal to me, either. Don't you have something that doesn't require the use of garden tools?"

"How about burning?"

Hallie shook her head. "I'm looking for something a little less violent. Neater and easier."

"Well, there's the sock method," Newton suggested.

By his tone Hallie could tell he didn't put much faith in that particular option. She was beginning to believe he'd rather fancied attacking Tris with a shovel himself. The notion brought a smile to her lips.

"But it doesn't work on every vampire," Newton added.

"The sock method?" Hallie asked. "That sounds like something I might like."

"You must steal the left sock of the vampire," Newton explained carefully. "Fill it with soil, or dirt from the grave. Then throw it outside the village limits, into a river if you can."

"We don't have a river. Would the ocean do?"

Newton shrugged. "Perhaps. I could do a little more research for you to find out."

"And will any grave do?"

Rubbing his chin, Newton thought about her question for a long moment. "I would suspect it would have to be dirt from Mr. Tristan's grave."

"Hmm," Hallie said. "That could cause a problem since I'm not sure Mr. Tristan has a grave."

"He has a coffin," Newton said.

"Thank you, Patience and Prudence," Hallie muttered beneath her breath.

"You could tear a small bit from the lining of the coffin and put that in the sock. Technically, it would be the same as dirt from his grave."

Hallie reached over the registration desk and patted Newton on the arm again. "Thank you for the information, Newton. I appreciate your concern. But I think I'll be able to handle anything Mr. Tristan sends my way."

Newton sniffled. "Are you sure?"

"Positive," Hallie replied. "Now, perhaps you'd best find your group. I'm not sure they'll know what they're doing without their president. I have to get back to work."

Newton nodded, then grabbed his book from the couch and headed to the front door. When he closed it behind him, Hallie breathed a sigh of relief. Then, grabbing her reservation book and a stack of messages from the board, she set off in search of her aunts. Obviously, her warnings about spreading gossip had gone unheeded.

She found them both in the small linen room behind the kitchen. The room, once one of three pantries, now housed the washer and dryer, an ironing board, and shelves for the inn's stock of linens. The aunts chattered to each other as they folded sheets.

Hallie watched them for a long moment, then decided she didn't have the energy to start another discussion about Edward Tristan. Besides, after his boorish behavior, she'd just as soon forget the man.

"Hallie, you're here," Prudence said, looking up from her work. "We've almost finished with the bed linens. The towels are done. And Sister and I have to get down to the town hall. We've got a rehearsal for our grand production tonight."

"Go ahead," Hallie said, waving them off. "I'll finish the bed linens for you."

They smiled and looked at each other, then scurried out of the laundry room. Patience stopped in the middle of the kitchen and turned back to Hallie. "I forgot to mention that Mr. Tristan stopped by the house last night. He asked if it would be possible to do his laundry."

Hallie raised her eyebrow. "What did you tell him?"

"His laundry is in the dryer. When it's finished, you'll fold it and return it to him, won't you?"

Hallie forced a smile and nodded. Satisfied that all her chores had been attended to, Patience hurried after her sister. Hallie sat down at the trestle table and opened her reservation book, then methodically went through her stack of pink message slips.

But Newton's words niggled at her mind and a few minutes later she stood and walked into the linen room. The empty laundry basket sat in front of the dryer. She opened the door and reached inside to touch his clothes. Everything seemed dry, so she pulled them out and dumped them in the basket, then hefted the basket up and carried it to the table.

The basket was filled with Tristan's customary black; black jeans, black turtlenecks and shirts. As she folded each piece of clothing, smoothing her hands over the warm fabric, she felt an odd, almost intimate connection to him, as if he were here with her, but not.

Hallie grabbed one of his shirts and pressed it to her nose, trying to detect the scent of his cologne on the collar. She closed her eyes and inhaled, then smiled to herself as a trace of the scent touched her nose.

She carefully folded the shirt and placed it on a stack, then reached into the basket again. Her breath caught in her throat as she pulled out a pair of boxers, black with a tiny red pattern. Hallie held them out in front of her and tried to imagine Tris dressed in nothing more.

An image of him flashed in her mind, bare-chested, the boxers hugging his narrow waist and hips. Pushing the thought aside, she quickly folded the boxers and reached into the basket again. This time, she withdrew a black sock.

A smile curled the corners of her mouth as she stared at the sock. "The left sock of a vampire," she repeated. She examined the sock more closely. "But is this the right or the left?" she murmured.

Hallie dug through the basket and pulled out eleven identical black socks, piling them in front of her. "How am I supposed to know which socks are the lefts?"

She considered the dilemma for a long time, weighing the odds of choosing the correct sock. In the end, she scooped up the whole pile and hurriedly headed for her bedroom. She'd hide them all there until she had a chance to complete the next step in her vampire eradication plan.

As she shoved her dresser drawer shut, the socks safely hidden inside, Hallie smiled in satisfaction. Whether Mr. Tristan was a vampire, or just an ordinary man, Hallie would use everything at her disposal to resist him. She had to, for the man had a powerful hold over her, a hold that could only cause her heartache when it came time for him to leave Egg Harbor.

"WHAT IS *wrong* with me?"

Hallie sat up in bed and groaned, covering her face with her hands. She'd had the dream again, the same dream that seemed to recur every time she fell asleep.

With a soft curse, she untangled her legs from the twisted bedsheet and unwrapped her nightgown from around her hips. The room seemed unnaturally hot and a thin sheen of perspiration broke out on her forehead. She crawled out of bed and walked over to the radiator, certain that it must be throwing off more heat than usual. But it was cool to the touch.

Fanning her face with her hand, she paced the floor at the end of the bed. This had to stop, these disturbing dreams of a man she could never have. She didn't need him! She didn't want him!

Then why couldn't she put him out of her mind? What was this power he seemed to hold over her? Hallie stopped short and ran her hands through her hair. Slowly she turned and hurried to her dresser. Tris's socks were exactly where she had left them. Hallie pulled one out, then shoved the drawer shut.

The parlor was dark and eerily silent as she tugged on her boots and shrugged into her jacket. The mantel clock chimed and Hallie counted along. Midnight. What better time to take care of such business? She grabbed her flashlight, then opened the front door.

A damp wind off the Atlantic sent a shiver coursing through her limbs as she stepped off the front porch. She made her way around the corner of the house, then tried to find the exact spot in the garden where she and Tris had stood together last.

Hallie made an educated guess, then bent and scooped up a handful of dirt. She carefully funneled it into the sock. "It may not be from a vampire's grave, but it's as close as I'm going to get tonight," she murmured to herself.

She snatched up the flashlight and headed toward the bluff. This was all her fault. If she'd have told Edward Tristan to leave when his two weeks were up, maybe she wouldn't still be so preoccupied with the man. But like a fool, she'd agreed to let him stay on at the Widow's Walk.

Was it really because she wanted the extra income? Or was there another reason, a reason she couldn't even admit to herself? Sure, she found him attractive, as would any woman whose sexual drive had been stuck in "Park" for as long as hers had. But this obsession of hers had gotten out of hand! She hadn't slept through the night since he'd arrived.

"It's not my fault," she said as she approached the bluff. "*He's* the one who is doing this to *me.*"

She held the sock filled with dirt in her hand. Then, with a swift and sure movement from her stone-skipping days as a child, she threw it out over the bluff and into the roiling surf below. Backing away from the rocky edge, she closed her eyes and said a silent prayer. "Stay out of my dreams, Edward Tristan. And stay out of my life."

Shivering, she turned around to head back for the house, but her return was stopped by a tall figure standing in her way. He grabbed her shoulders and looked down into her eyes.

"Hello, Hallie," Tris said. "What are you doing out here at this hour?"

Hallie sucked in a sharp breath and tried to still a shiver of apprehension. So much for the sock method. It had kept Tris away from her for all of three or four seconds. At this rate, a good night's sleep would require several thousand socks.

She twisted out of his grasp. "I—I couldn't sleep," she said, clutching her jacket more tightly around her.

"Dreaming of me?" he teased.

"Indigestion," she said. "What are you doing here?"

"I stopped by the house, looking for you," he explained as he bent, picked up his lantern and held it up to her face. "I thought you might still be up."

She tipped her flashlight until it illuminated his handsome face. "*You* were looking for *me?*"

"Actually, I was looking for your aunts, but they'd already retired for the evening."

"My aunts? What did you want with Patience and Prudence?"

Tris frowned, then shook his head. "It's the strangest thing. I asked them to do some of my laundry yesterday. I found the basket of clean clothes at the front door of the coach house, but all my socks were missing."

"Your socks?" Hallie said, swallowing hard.

"Yeah. I wanted to find out what they'd done with them."

Hallie shifted uneasily, then turned away from Tris and sat down on a large rock. "Why don't I check into it for you? The aunts can sometimes be very forgetful. They probably just neglected to put them back in the basket."

"Thank you," he said. "I'd appreciate that." He sat down beside her on the rock and placed the lantern between them. "So, why are you really out here?"

She gave him a sideways glance, trying to read his expression. The planes and angles of his face were lit by his flickering lantern and she detected a self-satisfied smirk curling his lips. "You think I came out here because I knew you'd be here?" she asked in disbelief.

"Did you?" Tris asked.

"The size of your ego is only exceeded by your amazing need for self-delusion. I couldn't sleep. I needed some fresh air."

"You did say you were going to stay away from me," Tris said. "Or did I misunderstand?"

Hallie stood and faced him, her arms braced on her hips. "I was out here first."

"You were waiting for me," he countered.

"You're the one who came to me! I was just sitting here, content to be alone."

"You're not alone now."

"So why don't you just leave?"

He didn't take her advice. Instead he just shook his head and chuckled softly. "You're the most stubborn woman I've ever met, Hallie Tyler," he said.

Hallie stared at him, her jaw tight. "Just because I don't succumb to your considerable charms?"

"Hallie, you can't ignore what's happening between us."

"I certainly can, if there's *nothing* going on between us."

He reached out and grabbed her hand. "But there is. I can see it in your eyes every time I touch you."

Hallie yanked her fingers out of his and stuck her hand in her pocket, making a fist until the warmth of his touch dissipated. "It's that cologne you wear. It makes my eyes water."

"Why don't you give us a chance? See just where all of this takes us? Aren't you the least bit curious?"

"I know where it will take us," Hallie replied. "And I don't want to go there."

"What are you afraid of?" he asked.

She glared at him wordlessly.

"Come on, Hallie," he said softly. "Talk to me."

She drew a deep breath, wondering if anything she said to him would make him see her point. "I've been alone for a long time," she explained. "And I like it."

He reached out and ran his palm along her arm. "You don't need to tell me what it's like to be alone, Hallie. I've been alone since I was a kid."

"I'm used to doing things for myself," she said, a hint of defensiveness in her voice. "My father died when I was eighteen and my mother, when I was nineteen. They left me enough money to go to college and maintain the house and help the aunts along. But it only took six years for the money to run out. I was two years behind with the taxes and the house needed work, so I came back here to make a life for myself."

"And you had to give up your life in Boston. And the man you wanted to marry."

"I wanted to come back," she said. "This was all I had left of my parents. This house and all the memories that went with it."

Tris stared deep into her eyes, a gaze that seemed to penetrate her very soul. "Is that why you want everything to stay the same, Hallie? So that you can preserve your memories?"

She pressed her lips into a tight line and shook her head. "No!" she snapped. "I just want to make sure that if I ever have a family of my own, there will be something left of the Tylers and Egg Harbor for them to appreciate."

"But you can't hope to have a family if you're determined to live life on your own."

She sighed, knowing the truth in his words. "For now, I'm the only one I can depend on. The aunts are counting on me. They have nothing left except a little social security. If it weren't for me, they'd be living on the streets. They're my responsibility now and so is the house."

Tris cursed softly. "So you'll sacrifice your life for them? And for the memories of your family? What about *you*, Hallie? Don't you deserve some happiness?"

"I *am* happy," she replied, trying hard to believe her own words.

"Are you?"

She laughed softly. "What? Do you think you're the one to sweep me off my feet and take care of all my troubles? Well you're not, Edward Tristan. I'm a big girl and I stopped believing in fairy tales a long time ago."

He stood and grabbed her arms. "I just think you should give us a chance, Hallie."

"And what about when it's time for you to go back to your real life? You're just a guest here, Mr. Tristan. You don't have any roots here, so there's no reason for you to stay."

"There's you," he said.

"Don't be ridiculous," she said. "We barely know each other."

"I intend to change that," Tris said. He bent closer and brushed his lips against hers, a gesture so simple and so fleeting at first she thought she'd imagined it.

Hallie wanted to run, to pull herself from his embrace and return to the safety of the inn. But as she stared into his intense gaze, she felt as if she were paralyzed, as if the only nerves alive in her body were those that tingled beneath his touch.

She opened her mouth to warn him off, but no words would come. Her thoughts were a mass of confusion, desire jumbled with a quickly fading resolve. He kissed her again, this time more deeply and she knew she was lost, unable to fight her own passion.

He pushed the front of her jacket open and ran his warm palms along her stomach and up her sides. She moaned softly beneath his mouth, pressing herself against his hands until it felt as if the thin fabric of her nightgown had disappeared and he touched her bare skin.

His hands cupped her breasts and his thumbs brushed against her nipples, the cold and his touch drawing them to taut peaks. Waves of sensation coursed through her body, heating her skin until she felt as if she were on fire.

"You can't deny it forever, Hallie," he whispered, his breath soft against her ear. "You will come to me. You can't resist me."

Then he suddenly stepped away from her, letting his hands drop to his sides. "Good night, Hallie."

She watched in disbelief as he turned on his heel and headed back toward the coach house. The cold wind blowing off the Atlantic whipped at her jacket, cooling her skin until her teeth chattered uncontrollably.

"Stay away from me, Edward Tristan!" she shouted after him. "Stay away!"

He turned back to her and shook his head. "Playing it safe isn't living, Hallie," he said, his words piercing the stiff wind. "It's merely existing."

With a curse, Hallie turned away from him and stared stubbornly out at the sea. Her gaze remained fixed on the ocean a long time after Tris left. In the distance, she watched the Bellsport lighthouse blink its warning to ships along the coast. A beacon in the dark, the light had always given her a sense of security, a knowledge of who she was and of the purpose in her life.

But now she felt like a ship lost in the fog. No matter how hard she searched for a safe harbor, there was none to be found. No matter where she turned, she risked crashing against the rocks of the coast or sinking into the dark depths of the sea.

She'd set a straight and true course for her life, but since Edward Tristan had arrived, that life had taken so many twists and turns she wasn't sure where she was headed. And always, there was his power over her, like an undertow, dragging her away from her purpose.

Was she really happy with the way her life had turned out, so safe yet so ordinary? Or was this excitement that Tris generated what she really wanted? Hallie closed her eyes and tipped her head back, Tris's last words echoing through her head.

Perhaps he was right. Perhaps it was time for her to take a few risks in her life.

6

"HE'S VERY CHARMING . . . for a vampire."

Hallie stood in the wide archway between the front parlor and the dining room, taking in the chaos that reigned beneath her aunts' careful watch. Paint-spattered newspapers were scattered over the worn Aubusson carpet. Five or six of the townsfolk worked diligently on huge pieces of canvas and rickety old furniture. Hallie's carefully chosen antique tables and chairs had been pushed back against the walls haphazardly.

"What have you done to my dining room?" she cried.

Patience and Prudence glanced over their shoulders and beamed at her. "Hallie! You're back! Did you get all your shopping done in Bangor?"

"Yes, I'm back. And it looks like I should never have left. What's going on in here?"

"We're working on the scenery and props for our grand production," Patience said, clasping her hands in front of her to contain her excitement.

Prudence nodded. "Isn't it wonderful? So many people are willing to help!" she added. "It's going to be a rousing success!"

Hallie raked her fingers through her hair, then winced as Hester Cromwell nearly tripped over a brimming can of purple paint, her dripping paint-brush coming perilously close to Hallie's favorite antique breakfront. "Couldn't you have done this down at the town hall?"

Patience shook her head. "The stove isn't working. There's an old squirrel's nest in the chimney," she said. "Besides, the paint would never dry properly in the cold. Silas promised to have the chimney swept by tomorrow night, but we needed to get started tonight. I think everything is going quite well, don't you, Sister?"

"Especially now that we have the help of Mr. Tristan!" Prudence said.

Hallie swallowed hard, then circled her aunts until she stood directly in front of them. "You asked Mr. Tristan to help you?" she asked, her gaze darting between the two older women.

Prudence shook her head. "Oh, no. He volunteered. We were discussing the play and he offered his help. I was just telling Sister that I found the man quite charming for a vampire."

Hallie gave her aunt an admonishing glare. "You know how I feel about that kind of talk," she warned. She glanced around the room, searching for Tris. "So, where is he?"

"He's not here right now, dear," Patience said, reaching out and grasping Hallie's hand. "He and Prissy Pemberton went into the village to get more paintbrushes." She looked at her watch. "They've been gone for quite some time now, Sister. I wonder what's happened to them?"

"He needn't have driven her," Prudence said disapprovingly. "But that Prissy has been hanging on his every word all evening. I think she fancies our Mr. Tristan."

"She fancies anything in pants," Patience replied.

Prudence gasped and covered her mouth with her hand. "Sister! The way you talk! Mother would not countenance talk like that."

Patience clucked her tongue and shook her head. "Everyone in town knows that our mayor's favorite daughter is nothing but a brazen hussy. She's gone through every eligible man in Egg Harbor. She's had to move on to out-of-towners, now."

"Still, we must be more charitable toward our neighbors."

Patience crossed her arms in front of her. "Charitable? It would serve her right if Mr. Tristan gave her a little nip on the neck. In fact, he could bite her entire empty head off and no one would blame him in the least."

Hallie sighed and held up her hands to silence their chattering. "Mr. Tristan is not going to bite Prissy on the—"

"Hello, everyone!" The perky greeting reverberated through the first floor of the inn and Hallie ground her teeth. She and her aunts turned around and watched Prissy Pemberton sweep through the front door, her arm linked through Tris's.

Prissy had been head cheerleader at Egg Harbor High during all four years that Hallie had attended. She'd also been prom queen, homecoming queen and drum majorette. The only place Hallie had been able to best her was in grades, for Prissy had always preferred boys and social pursuits to higher education.

Hallie had finally escaped Prissy when she'd moved to Boston to attend college. Boston was the one place

Prissy wouldn't follow. Prissy much preferred being the prettiest piranha in a very small pond.

Hallie studied her old nemesis as she and Tris strolled through the parlor. Prissy's hair, once naturally blond, was now bleached by Melba down at the Snip 'n' Shear, and her curves, the envy of every girl at Egg Harbor High, were stuffed into skintight jeans and a sweater several sizes too small. But Prissy had maintained her bubbly personality and her indisputable way with men—even through three marriages and three subsequent divorces.

"We're back!" she cried as they approached Patience and Prudence. "And we've got just scads of brushes, don't we, Trissy?" She gave his arm a squeeze, pressing it against her ample bosom.

"Trissy?" Hallie said.

Tris grinned and quirked an eyebrow up at Hallie. "Miss Tyler, I didn't expect you to be here. I didn't think you were interested in supporting the Vampire Festival."

"Hallie's always got a bug in her undies about something," Prissy said with a haughty sniff. "No wonder you're still an old spinster, Hallie Tyler!" She giggled then, in that irritating, artificial way that Hallie had always detested.

Hallie opened her mouth to spit an equally insulting comment back at Prissy, but Tris interrupted her. "Prissy, why don't you take those paintbrushes into the dining room and get started. I'll join you there in just a moment."

Prissy gazed up at him and batted her eyelashes. "Don't be too long, Trissy," she cooed.

Hallie watched as Prissy sashayed her way past her, hips swinging provocatively. Then she turned her gaze back to Tris who was admiring Prissy's rather overblown exit.

"Prissy and Trissy," Hallie mocked. "That's just too sweet. I do believe I used to know a pair of poodles with those very same names."

Tris stepped closer and bent his head so that his words remained between the two of them. "You sound jealous," he murmured.

Hallie stepped back. "Jealous?" she hissed. "Of Prissy Pemberton? Oh, yes, I've always dreamed of being exactly like her. Then I could attract the attention of men with entirely *no* taste in women." Hallie put her finger on her cheek and feigned a surprised look. "Now, that would be a man like you, wouldn't it?"

Tris chuckled and tapped her on the tip of her nose with his finger. "Green looks good on you, Hallie. It's definitely your color." With that, he turned and walked into the dining room, then bent next to Prissy as she dabbed paint on a backdrop.

Hallie rubbed her nose in irritation, then glanced down at the clothes she wore. Only then did she realize she wasn't wearing a stitch of green. Suddenly, Tris's comment was revealed for what it truly was—an insult as grating as Prissy's!

"I'm not jealous of Prissy Pemberton," she muttered beneath her breath.

"Of course you're not, dear."

Hallie turned at the sound of Prudence's voice beside her. She gave her aunt an impatient glance.

"What would you have to be jealous of?" Patience asked as she stepped to Hallie's other side.

Hallie crossed her arms in front of her. "What is she doing here anyway?" she grumbled. "I would think she'd be the last person you'd want working on your play."

"Well, we had to have a virgin," Patience said in a matter-of-fact tone. "And she was the closest we could find."

Hallie scoffed. "Prissy Pemberton is playing the virgin in your play? Isn't that a bit of stretch for her?"

"We didn't have much choice, dear," Prudence explained. "You wouldn't take the part. All the others that auditioned were well past the age of innocence."

Hallie's gaze drifted over to the cozy little scene between Tris and Prissy. His hand now covered hers as he helped her paint a corner of the scenery. She wriggled closer to him until her body pressed against his. "I've got work to do," Hallie said, her jaw tight. "Please make sure this mess is cleaned up before everyone leaves."

With that, she turned and headed back into the parlor. She sat down behind the front desk and distractedly flipped through her messages before she glanced back into the dining room. From her vantage point, she could just barely see Tris. He'd left Prissy's side and was now helping her aunts move a large chair into the center of the room.

He listened patiently to their directions, moving it at least four times before they were satisfied. Then he graced them with an indulgent smile before all three of them then bent over a can of paint. Hallie watched as Tris mixed in colors to their exacting instructions, dabbing a bit on the chair every few minutes until they'd achieved the perfect shade.

She smiled to herself. Her aunts were right. He could be quite charming when he wanted to be. And it was awfully sweet of him to volunteer his time to help Patience and Prudence. There were not many men she'd known who had the fortitude to put up with the two imperious eighty-year-old women.

Bracing her chin in her hand, Hallie looked back down at her reservation book. But no matter how hard she tried to concentrate on work, her gaze constantly returned to the dining room—and to Edward Tristan.

She really shouldn't care at all that he had turned his attentions to Prissy Pemberton. After all, if he had someone else to occupy his time, maybe he'd leave her alone. Hallie cursed softly. Then why *did* she care? Why did every smile Tris turned on that bubble-headed bimbo set her teeth on edge?

Perhaps she cared more about the man than she wanted to admit. Tris was handsome and mysterious and he'd brought some real excitement into her life for the first time in a very long time. And she'd come to look forward to the occasions when he turned his charm in her direction.

So why had she been so reluctant to let it go any further? Was she simply being practical? Or was she afraid of risking her heart for a man she barely knew? She knew he possessed a startling power over her, the power to dissolve all her doubts and fears with a single touch, to make her body come alive with a passion she'd never felt before.

She hungered to be close to him, yet she sensed a danger in allowing herself that pleasure. She longed to know him better, yet she wasn't sure of the man she might find behind those pale blue eyes. Since the day she'd met him, she had tried with all her might to resist her attraction to him, to deny his power over her, but just how much longer could she stay away from him? How much longer could her mind fight what her body desired?

Hallie closed her eyes, but an image of Tris remained indelibly burned in her consciousness. Maybe it *was* time to take a risk, to trust her heart to a man again. She wanted to love and to be loved, but if she never took a chance again, she'd never know what she might have missed.

She looked across the room at him, her gaze drifting along his lean body. Tris could be the man who might love her for the rest of her life. Or he might be the man who could shatter her heart forever.

Perhaps it was time to find out which it really was.

TRIS STARED at the blinking cursor on his computer screen, then leaned back in his chair and linked his hands behind his head. His eyes drifted over the words he had just written, an image of the story playing in his head like a silent movie.

His heroine had become Hallie, sweet and innocent, stalked by an immortal that would let nothing stand in the way of his unquenchable thirst and his over-whelming desire. Filled with menace and evil, the vampire wanted her with every breath he took, letting nothing stand in his way—a concept that Tris seemed to have no trouble conveying. He was beginning to un-derstand how the poor guy felt.

In his own mind, he had become the vampire, ob-sessed with the soft sound of her voice and the tanta-lizing silkiness of her skin, the almost constant need to touch her. He wanted her, so much he could barely stand to be near her. But the lines between fiction and life had begun to blur and he wasn't sure of where to redraw them.

Was it Hallie he really wanted? Or was it the woman he'd created on the page, a woman who had become almost real to him? Tris closed his eyes and shook his head. They were one and the same, weren't they?

He'd created his character in Hallie's image, infusing her with all the qualities he knew Hallie possessed—intelligence, determination, courage. But his heroine was malleable, acting on his every whim with no complaint or resistance. Unfortunately, Hallie was a lot more stubborn than the character rattling around in his head.

Still, that only made him want her more. She was a real woman with faults and foibles, qualities he found just as fascinating as everything else about her. No, he didn't want a mere character who existed only on paper. He wanted a living, breathing woman, a woman who drove him to distraction with her every smile, her every touch.

But did she want *him?* On the page, it was so easy to create reciprocal desire. It was much harder in real life. Hallie had become a challenge and, like the vampire, he felt as if he couldn't stop until he possessed her. Tris twisted his head as he rubbed a kink out of his neck. Perhaps he was more like the vampire than he thought—dangerous, unscrupulous, willing to do anything to have what he wanted.

And in the end, what could he really offer Hallie? Life with Tristan Montgomery and his rabid fans held about as much appeal as a future without sunlight. Tris cursed softly. A future? A future with Hallie Tyler was just about as likely as an appearance of old Uncle Nicholas. She wanted nothing to do with him . . . or did she?

His mind wandered back to the events of earlier that evening, stopping to linger over the look on Hallie's face when he had left the inn to drive Prissy Pemberton home. He'd never guessed Hallie to be the jealous type. But the glare she'd sent him from her place behind the front desk was enough to tell him that she didn't approve of Prissy, or his interest in her.

Tris smiled. What interest? Prissy was an emptyheaded flirt who was only interested in Tris's financial situation and his subsequent ability to buy a woman whatever her fickle little heart desired. He'd met plenty of women exactly like her, perhaps not quite as obvious, but just as mercenary.

Hallie needn't have been concerned, but he'd taken great pleasure in the fact that she was. He only wished he had thought of tweaking Hallie's jealousy earlier, especially after experiencing his own irritated reaction to seeing Newton and Hallie together.

Would she ever admit her attraction to him? Or were they doomed to be at odds forever? Hallie was the most obstinate woman he'd ever known, but after tonight Tris wondered if her iron resolve wasn't beginning to crumble. She'd been alone for so long, perhaps she had simply resigned herself to solitary life and never considered the alternatives.

Tris turned back to his work but had only typed a few words when a sharp rap sounded at the door. He hesitated before getting up to answer it, wondering if Prissy had decided to come back and make one last attempt to lure him into bed. He pulled the door open a crack only to find Hallie standing on the other side, a stack of towels in her arms.

He fought the urge to smile in satisfaction. "Miss Tyler," he said, bracing his shoulder against the edge of the door. "What brings you out so late at night?"

"Is it late?" She craned her neck and tried to peer inside the coach house, but he stood squarely in her way, unmoving. "I thought you might need some fresh towels."

"I have plenty of clean towels," Tris said. "Although I'm still a little short on socks."

She forced a smile. "I'm still looking into that situation. If we've somehow lost your socks, we'll certainly replace them for you. I—I can't imagine what happened to them."

"Was there something else you wanted, Miss Tyler?" Tris asked.

"Actually, there is," she said. "But if you're busy..."

"Busy?" Tris asked.

She shifted uneasily and he saw a blush creep up her already rosy cheeks. "I meant, if you're entertaining company, I can come back."

"Company?" Tris interrupted.

She sighed and shot him an irritated look. "Do you want me to come right out and ask?" she said, her voice nearly a whisper. "Would that make you happy? All right, I will. Is Prissy here with you or are you alone?"

Tris chuckled. "I took Prissy home hours ago," he replied. "Now, what was it you wanted?"

She tipped her chin up defiantly. "I wanted to know if you'd like to take a walk with me. I think we have some things to discuss."

"About the disappearance of my socks?" he asked in mock seriousness.

"Do you have to make this so difficult?" Hallie snapped.

Tris wiped the grin from his face and gazed at her intently. "All right, what would you like to talk about?"

"About us," she said.

"Ah, my favorite subject," he said, grabbing the towels from her arms. "Let me get my coat."

She waited for him at the door, her eyes wide, her hands clutched in front of her. Whatever she had to tell him, the prospect had turned her into a nervous wreck. "I'd like to thank you for helping out my aunts," she said in a distracted voice. "They really appreciated it."

"I was happy to do it," Tris said as he shrugged into his coat. "They're quite a pair."

She gave him a wavering smile. "Yes, they are."

He joined her at the door, then pulled it shut behind him. He wanted to reach for her hand, but she seemed so tense that he knew she'd pull away. Instead they walked down the narrow path toward the inn without touching, her flashlight shining the way. "Where are we going?" he asked.

His words seemed to startle her and she glanced at him furtively. "I—I thought we could walk down into the village."

They spent the next ten minutes in utter silence, Hallie striding along purposefully as if he weren't there at all. When they finally reached the edge of town, she relaxed a bit. She flipped off her flashlight and they made their way through the fog-shrouded streets by the soft glow of the streetlights.

He heard her take a deep breath and then she turned to him. "You were right," she said softly, looking up at him with liquid eyes.

Tris smiled down at her. "That's nice to know. But what was I right about?"

"About me. About us," she said. She didn't say any more until they reached the waterfront. Tris didn't make an attempt to draw her out or to tease her any further. He sensed that she hovered on the edge of indecision, as if one wrong word from him would send her in the opposite direction. For now, it was best to proceed at Hallie's own pace. If he was lucky, he'd find out what was bothering her sometime before dawn.

They slowly walked down to the end of the pier. "Would you like to sit?" she asked, pointing to a bench.

"Sure," Tris replied.

They both sat on the bench, Hallie staying just out of the range of his touch. She stared out at the harbor, silent and uncertain, her face a mask of warring emotions, her body coiled as tightly as a spring.

"My father and I used to come down here and watch the lobster boats come in," she said, her hands folded on her lap. Another silence grew between them.

"What is it, Hallie?" he finally asked. "What did you want to discuss? Surely not lobster boats."

"I—I was wrong to ignore what was happening between us. You were right. I took the safe way out. I didn't want to risk getting hurt. But the fact is, I enjoy your company." She glanced over at him. "I—I like being with you. And I think that should count for something."

"So what does this mean, Hallie?"

"It means that I think it would be all right if we got to know each other a little better. If we spent more time together. Then maybe I'd be able to know for sure how I really feel."

"I think you already know," Tris said.

"I know how I feel—" She swallowed hard. "Physically. I—I mean, you're a very attractive man and that fact isn't lost on me. It's just that, I think there should be more than just a physical attraction between us before we—you know."

"Make love?" he asked.

She nodded, her head bobbing up and down nervously. "But it seems as if every time we're together we can't avoid our..." She paused. "Desire for each other."

"There's nothing wrong with that," Tris said.

"I know. But I'd like to think that there might be *more* between us. Unless—"

"Unless?"

She swallowed hard and glanced up at him. "Unless you don't think there's anything more. I mean, if all you're interested in is...you know, then you should tell me right away."

Tris reached out and cupped her cheek in his hand. "No, Hallie, that's not all I'm interested in."

She sighed deeply and smiled. "Good. That makes me feel much better."

"So what do you want to do?" he asked. "You tell me."

"I want to spend some time together, but I want to take things slowly."

"Slow can be very nice," Tris said. He paused. "So, can I hold your hand now, or would that be moving too fast?"

Hallie nodded and smiled. Tris twisted her delicate fingers through his, then tucked her hand in his coat pocket. She moved closer to him and rested her head on his shoulder as they stared out into the fog-shrouded harbor. A foghorn sounded in the distance and the lobster trawlers groaned at their moorings, but a strange peace had descended around them.

"How long will you stay in Egg Harbor?" she asked softly.

Tris squeezed her hand. "I'm not sure. I like it here and right now there's no reason for me to leave."

She glanced up at him. "Don't you have to go back to work soon?"

He shook his head. "What would you say if I told you I was independently wealthy?" he asked.

Hallie shrugged. "I'd wonder why you chose Egg Harbor for your vacation destination," she replied. "It's not exactly the French Riviera."

"But it is the Vampire Capital of the World," he said.

She frowned and he bumped against her shoulder playfully. "Perhaps it was fate," he said. "Perhaps I came here to meet you."

"My aunts were right. You are very charming."

Tris took a long breath, knowing that now was as good a time as any to tell her the truth about his identity. Sooner or later, he'd have to tell her that Edward Tristan was really Tristan Montgomery, bestselling novelist.

He'd just never expected to fall for Hallie the way he had, so fast—and so hard. He'd always had such control over his emotions and needs, especially when it came to women. But all that control simply dissolved when he looked into Hallie Tyler's eyes. He'd fallen, all right, and there wasn't a damn thing he could do about it.

He'd like to think that his identity and his career made absolutely no difference in what was happening between them. Here in Egg Harbor he'd become what he'd wanted to become—anonymous, a visitor who had left the complications of his life behind. He felt more himself in this small town than he'd been for years in Manhattan.

And he *had* told Hallie the truth, at least part of it. He was independently wealthy. Tris knew after he finished this book he wouldn't have to write another word for the rest of his life if he didn't want to. He'd invested his money well and could afford to live a comfortable existence in whatever place he chose.

In the end, he decided not to tell her, not to test the fragile bond that had been forged between them. If and when it became necessary, he would tell her, about his life in New York, about his career. But for now he'd remain Edward Tristan, the man that Hallie had begun to care for.

The man who had begun to care for her more than he'd ever thought possible.

HIS MOUTH WAS WARM and soft on hers, his kisses gently undermining her resolve in the same way the tides worked against a stalwart sandbar. They lay stretched out on the sofa in the coach house, Hallie's body pulled tight against his, his leg thrown possessively over her hip and his hand splayed across her backside. She wanted to stop the sweet torment, but she knew she couldn't. Instead she groaned inwardly and let the current of sensation sweep her away.

This all seemed so inevitable. Some nights they'd sit on the bluff and watch the ocean. Other nights they'd walk the silent streets of Egg Harbor. Still other nights, they'd sit in front of a cozy fire in the coach house. But no matter what they did during the evening, it all seemed to culminate in the moments they spent saying good-night.

At first it had been a casual wave at the door, then a simple kiss. But with every passing night, their farewell became more tantalizing and more passionate. She had tried to resist him, to backtrack to a more reasonable point, but it was impossible. She'd come to crave his kisses as much as she enjoyed his company.

To her relief, that was as far as they had gone—kissing. Very passionate, mind-numbing kissing, but kissing nonetheless. In deference to her wishes, Tris had managed to stop at that, though she could tell that at times he was reaching the limits of his self-control. As he pulled her beneath him and settled his hips against hers, she knew without a doubt that this was one of those times.

Gently, Hallie pushed at his shoulders until he dragged his mouth from hers and looked down into her eyes. The cloud of desire slowly cleared from his gaze and he sighed in resignation. "I guess it's time for you to go," he murmured before allowing himself one last, lingering kiss.

Hallie brushed her thumb along his moist lower lip then wriggled out from beneath him. She sat on the edge of the couch, smoothing the wrinkles from her clothes. "I have work to do. I've got to set the dining room for breakfast tomorrow morning and I have to start my bread dough tonight so it can rise. If I don't leave now, I might as well forget about getting any sleep tonight."

Tris pushed himself up and sat beside her, then took her hand and wove his fingers through hers. He studied their joined hands for a long time, contemplating what he was about to say. Finally, he glanced over at her and smiled. "You'd better go," he said.

She sensed he meant to say something else, but she was certain she really didn't want to hear it. He was about to tell her that he couldn't go on like this, that they couldn't continue to spend time together without taking the next step toward a physical relationship. It was only natural. He wanted to make love to her. And though she tried hard to deny it, she was almost sure that's what she wanted, as well.

But was she really ready for such a momentous shift in their relationship? Was she prepared for all the consequences that making love to him would bring? She cared about him, that much was clear. And he cared about her. But was that enough?

No, Hallie said to herself. It wasn't. Not nearly enough to ensure that she wouldn't be hurt in the end. She quickly stood and turned to him. "I guess I'll see you tomorrow," she said.

"I'm not going anywhere, Hallie," he replied, sinking back into the cushions of the sofa.

Hallie nodded, then walked to the door, his words reverberating in her head. As she pulled the door shut behind her, she leaned back for a moment and closed her eyes. If only she could see into the future, she'd know what to do, what path to take. But no one could do that. Sooner or later, everyone had to take a risk.

Hallie pushed away from the door and hurried down the path to the inn. Why did there have to be a risk? Why couldn't her decision be simple? She cared about him and he cared about her. That didn't mean they had to spend the rest of their lives together, did it?

A nagging fear twisted at her heart. It was easy to be indifferent now, but how would she feel after he'd abandoned her to return to his own life? She knew all too well what it felt like to lose someone she loved. It had taken her years to fill the emptiness that her parents' deaths had caused, to reconcile herself to the fact that she was alone in the world. Could she go through that again?

The kitchen was dark and silent when Hallie walked in. She slipped out of her coat and tossed it across the counter, then grabbed a stack of freshly starched napkins from the shelf in the laundry room.

As she stepped into the dimly lit dining room, she found Patience and Prudence sitting at a table near the large bay window. "What are you two doing up so late?" she asked. "It's nearly midnight."

They watched her silently while she deftly folded a napkin and placed it on the table closest to the kitchen door. They both took a casual sip of their tea and gave each other a meaningful look. Hallie raised her eyebrow, then shook her head. "How long do you two intend to sit there staring at me?"

They both carefully folded their hands in front of them, a gesture that didn't bode well for Hallie. Whenever the Sisters were bothered by something, they always felt it best to confront the problem with a family meeting over tea and cookies. She noticed a third cup on the table, obviously waiting for her arrival.

Patience spoke first. "How long did you intend to keep your assignations with Mr. Tristan a secret?"

Hallie stared down at the napkin on the table and busied herself with straightening the intricate folds. "'Assignations'? What 'assignations'?"

She knew perfectly well what assignations! She'd been meeting Tris every night for the past week and tonight had been no different. Her mind wandered back to the coach house, to the taste of his mouth against hers, to the flood of sensation that overwhelmed all her resolve.

"You've been sneaking out late at night and meeting him," Prudence accused, interrupting Hallie's thoughts.

Hallie looked up at them, frowning. "Have you been spying on me, as well?"

Patience clucked her tongue and shook her head, as if scolding a recalcitrant child. "Hallie, dear, we're only concerned for your well-being. This Mr. Tristan is a dangerous man."

He was dangerous, all right, Hallie mused. But not in the way the aunts thought. "Mr. Tristan is a very nice man," Hallie countered. "And if you two didn't have vampires on the brain, you'd be able to see that."

"This is the way it starts, Sister," Prudence said in a dismal tone. "Remember that poor Lucy Westenra in Mr. Stoker's book? She was seduced by the dark powers of the vampire and look what happened to her!"

"An innocent virgin," Patience said. "Just like our Hallie."

A napkin slipped out of Hallie's fingers and landed on the floor at her feet. She cursed silently and braced her hands on her hips, her temper pricked. "Tris is not a vampire," she began, her voice rising with each word,

"Lucy was a character in a book of *fiction*, and I am not a virgin!"

The Sisters' eyes went wide and a deep flush crept up their parchment cheeks. Their mouths fell open and snapped shut, like two fish tossed up on the rocks, and their hands fluttered back and forth between their teacups and their hair in birdlike gestures.

Hallie stifled a groan. So maybe she shouldn't have told them. But their meddling would have to stop, especially when it interfered with her social life. For the first time in years she'd met someone she was interested in, someone she desired and might even love someday. And he seemed genuinely interested in her. These things didn't happen everyday in Egg Harbor and she wouldn't let the Sisters ruin it with all their ridiculous gossip.

"I'm sorry I just blurted it out like that," Hallie said. "I didn't mean to upset your tender sensibilities. But I want you both to understand that this is none of your business. What I do and what I don't do with Mr. Tristan is up to me."

"Then it's already happened," Patience said, her words a mournful wail.

"Oh, Sister, we are too late," Prudence cried.

"Too late for what?" Hallie asked.

"He's . . . taken you," Patience said, reaching for her handkerchief to dab at her eyes.

"Ravished you," Prudence added, grabbing the handkerchief from her sister's hand.

"Made you one of his kind," Patience concluded.

Hallie frowned. "Who? Mr. Tristan?"

They both nodded solemnly.

Hallie gasped. "You think *I'm* a vampire now?"

They nodded again.

A chuckle grew in Hallie's throat until it burst forth in gales of laughter. She laughed so hard, tears came to her eyes. She pulled out a chair and sat down, trying to compose herself, but one look at the Sisters' stricken expressions brought it all back.

Gulping down deep breaths of air, Hallie finally calmed herself. She took a long sip of her lukewarm tea, then cleared her throat. "You think Mr. Tristan and I have had sex. You think he bit me on the neck and now I'm a vampire."

"This is all our fault," Patience said. "If we hadn't brought up that story about Uncle Nicholas, this never would have happened. That article would have never appeared in the *Times*. Mr. Tristan never would have come to Egg Harbor and he never would have debauched our darling Hallie."

"He didn't debauch me!" Hallie cried, dropping her teacup into the saucer. "Nothing has happened between Mr. Tristan and me. Not that I don't want it to, but that's also none of your business."

"Then you are still . . . pure?" Patience asked.

Hallie shook her head. "Ladies, if you'll remember, I lived with my fiancé in Boston."

They both looked at her, dumbfounded, their expressions blank.

"We shared an apartment *and* a bedroom," Hallie continued.

Patience shifted uneasily in her chair. "You mean..."

Hallie nodded.

"How many times?" Prudence inquired curiously.

"More than once," Hallie said.

They both leaned forward, their elbows braced on the table, their fingers twisting together nervously. "And was it . . ." Patience paused.

"Exciting?" Prudence finished. "Did he . . ."

"Seduce you?" Patience asked.

Hallie watched them suspiciously. "Why all the questions?"

"Well, darling," Patience explained, "we can't help but be a bit curious about the whole business. After all, Mother told us how awful it would be, but we've read many, many books which say just the opposite."

"And now we have someone who has firsthand knowledge," Prudence said cheerily. "So do tell us all the details. What is it really like? Who decides when it's time? And how do you know which clothes to remove and which to leave on? And do you talk while it's going on? And how do you know when it's over?"

Hallie looked back and forth between their expectant expressions. They actually wanted to know the details of her sex life? Somehow she couldn't imagine explaining something like this to her almost-eighty-year-old maiden aunts. But they seemed so earnest in their questions and they really didn't have a clue.

What was she supposed to tell them, that sex with her ex-fiancé, Jonathan, was never very exciting? That she'd always wondered whether there shouldn't be more passion and excitement in their relationship?

Or should she tell them how just the thought of Tris's touch sent shivers of desire racing to her core? Or how fantasies about making love to him invaded her dreams nearly every night?

"It was exactly like all the books said," Hallie finally replied with an exaggerated nod. "*Exactly*. Whatever you've read about it is absolutely true."

"I told you, Sister," Patience said. "One must leave the nightclothes on and the lights out!"

Patience straightened in her chair and put on a stern expression, ignoring her twin sister's satisfied smile. "Well, Sister, if all those books are true, then you and I were right to worry about Hallie and Mr. Tristan." She turned to Hallie. "Men can be powerfully seductive creatures. We've seen the way you look at Mr. Tristan and it is quite clear from how he looks at you that he has seduction in mind."

Hallie looked back and forth at her aunts. "How does he look at me?" Obviously the aunts had been keeping her under *very* close watch. Even she hadn't noticed how Tris looked at her. He always seemed in such utter control of his emotions. Could they be right? Could he actually want her as much as she wanted him? If he did, why hadn't he made a single move to take her to his bed?

"His hooded eyes are slaked with the fires of desire," Prudence said dramatically.

"His body is taut with barely controlled passion, ready to burst forth in a maelstrom of torrid need," Patience added.

"He wants to possess you, Hallie," they both said. "In both body and soul."

"So what if he does?" she countered with a shrug. "Maybe I want him. He's a very attractive man. And I haven't had a man in a very long time."

Prudence reached out and grabbed Hallie's hand. "But Mr. Tristan is not the kind of man for you. He's dangerous."

Hallie groaned and covered her face with her hands. "Are we back to that again?" She dropped her hands and looked directly at her aunts. "He's not dead or undead. Mr. Tristan is very much alive. Some rather strange circumstances have conspired to make you believe he's something that he's not. And I'm sure there's a logical explanation for all of it. But until Tris offers one, I'm not going to press him. He's a very private man and I respect that."

"A very private man with his own coffin," Prudence said.

Hallie opened her mouth to reply to Prudence, then snapped it shut. Her aunt was right. She hadn't quite figured out the coffin. Tris had treated it as if it were some practical joke a friend had played on him. After a while, she'd just accepted that explanation. But had she been right to brush it off so easily?

"And what about his other habits?" Patience said.

"Would you like to know what I think?" Hallie asked. "I think Tris came here to escape from some problem. Maybe it was another woman or maybe something awful happened in his life. He seems to be under a great deal of stress and he doesn't sleep at night. He also doesn't eat much. Most people who are stressed don't maintain a healthy diet."

"He doesn't eat at all," Prudence said.

"I'm sure he does," Hallie retorted. "You've just never seen him eat."

Prudence raised her brow dubiously. "And have you ever seen him during daylight hours?"

"Of course," Hallie lied. "Several times. And isn't sunlight supposed to kill vampires?"

"That is not true of all vampire species," Patience said. "Some can tolerate small amounts of sunlight. And Bulgarian Gypsy vampires eat real food all the time."

Hallie felt her temper rise again at her aunts' intractability. They seemed to have an answer for everything. "What do I have to say to you to make you forget this silly notion you have about Mr. Tristan?"

"I'm afraid we cannot be convinced," Patience said stubbornly.

"Then we're at a stalemate, because I'm not going to stop seeing Tris. I'm . . . interested in him. And he's interested in me."

Patience reached into her pocket and withdrew a long gold chain, with a beautifully jeweled cross. She held it out to Hallie. "This was Mother's. She wore it on her wedding day. It will protect you, Hallie. We want you to wear it."

Hallie slowly reached out for the lovely piece, fingering the delicate filigree work that surrounded the old garnets. "If I wear this, will you two stop badgering me about Mr. Tristan?"

The Sisters looked at each other, then at Hallie, before nodding. "If you promise to wear it at all times," Patience said. "Never take it off."

"Never," Prudence repeated.

Hallie took a long breath, then acquiesced. "All right. I'll wear this and *you'll* stop your spying." She stood, then circled the table and gave both her aunts a hug. "Please, don't worry about me. I'm a big girl and I can take care of myself. And Mr. Tristan is no one to be afraid of."

With that, Hallie pulled the chain over her head and adjusted the cross around her neck. She looked down at the necklace as it glittered just above her breasts. If only a simple piece of jewelry could protect her.

She had already surrendered her heart to Tris. If she surrendered her body, would she ever be able to let him go?

7

BANNERS FESTOONED the main street of Egg Harbor, snapping in the brisk ocean breeze above Hallie's head. Each banner shouted a welcome to vampire lovers, due to arrive for the festival in less than a week.

Everyone had gotten into the act, from Melba at the beauty shop who offered a special price on black dye jobs to Wilber, owner of the lumberyard, who was selling wooden stakes for a dollar apiece. Images of vampires stared out from nearly every shop window, menacing black-caped figures with pale faces and vicious eyeteeth. And Hallie had heard that the Ladies' League had just finished new vampire costumes for the high school marching band to wear for the kickoff parade down Main Street.

Hallie walked toward the waterfront, wondering with every step how her life could have changed so much in such a short time. Just over a month ago the review of the Widow's Walk Inn had appeared in the *New York Times* and since then, her calm and orderly professional life had turned upside down. The town had gone berserk with vampire mania. And Edward Tristan had stepped through the front door of the inn, throwing her personal life into chaos, as well.

She'd thought that getting to know Tris a little better would end all her confusion. But the more time they spent together, the more difficult it was for her to determine her true feelings for him. She wanted him more than she'd ever wanted a man before. But what was driving that need? Was it the depth of her feelings or simply a shallow physical desire?

An image of Tristan drifted through her mind and she lingered over it for a long moment. She could recall his features with startling clarity, his pale blue eyes, his long, dark hair, the feel of his lips on hers and the sound of his breath against her ear. When she was with him, she wanted nothing more than to stare at him for endless hours, to listen to his smooth, seductive voice and enjoy his soft touch.

So there *was* an overwhelming physical component to her feelings for him. Still, there had to be more. But what? And would they have time to find it? Every so often she would wonder when the real world would finally intrude upon them. When would Tris tire of Egg Harbor and pack his bags to head back home?

He couldn't live in her coach house forever, although he'd made no move to leave. Sooner or later, they would both come to a crossroads in their relationship. They'd have to face their true feelings and deal with the future—or a lack of one.

Right now, there was no future. She lived entirely in the present, enjoying their time together and refusing to believe that it might come to an end. Every time she thought about Tristan leaving Egg Harbor, a nagging emptiness settled around her heart, an emptiness that was all too familiar to her.

Hallie scolded herself inwardly and pushed her fears aside, trying to concentrate on her plans for this evening. In the past week, she'd shown Tris just how wonderful small-town life could be and tonight would be no different.

Hallie looked up at the sign for Big John's Bait Shop, pushed the front door open and stepped inside. She had visited the store so many times as a girl, walking downtown with her father to purchase a carton of worms before spending a lazy afternoon fishing at a nearby millpond.

Big John, a retired lobster man, now made a living supplying the recreational fishermen of the town with worms, minnows, and deep sea fishing bait. His shop was a gathering place for the men of the town and as Hallie stepped up to the counter, she noticed that most of the town council sat gathered around the potbellied stove, their booted feet braced on the base.

"Mornin', Hallie," Silas called.

Hallie groaned softly. The last person she wanted to run into this morning was Silas Pemberton. "Good morning, Silas."

The mayor cleared his throat and leaned back in his chair. "So, what do you think of our festival plans so far?"

"Very... festive," she said.

"Ah-yup. We're looking forward to a real big crowd."

"I'm sure you are," she said. "Big John, I'd like one of those clam-digging forks and a galvanized bucket."

"I guess you can't fight progress, eh, Hallie?"

Hallie paid for her purchases, then walked over to the little group gathered around the stove. She knew she should have just walked out, refusing to take Silas's bait. But she couldn't. "If you think destroying the beauty and serenity of Egg Harbor is progress, then all I can say is I'll fight you every step of the way, Silas. You and your cronies on the town board."

"Why are you fightin' us, missy?" he snapped, tipping down his chair with a thud.

"Doesn't it bother you that you're bringing all these people here under false pretenses? There never has been a vampire in my family or in Egg Harbor. The whole story about Nicholas Tyler is just a silly legend."

Silas grunted. "Legend or not, there are plenty of folks who are coming here to look for old Nick. If you were smart, you'd make sure he puts in an appearance."

"Nicholas Tyler will not put in an appearance, because he's dead!" Hallie said. "He's been dead for over seventy years. And once your vampire lovers learn this is all a hoax, I think they'll stay home."

"Unless you've got proof, you'd better keep your opinions to yourself," Silas said, shaking his finger at her. "Lots of folks in town have invested time and money in this festival. I don't want you spoiling it for everyone."

Hallie took a deep breath and tried to school her temper. The last thing she wanted to do today was get into a long-winded argument about tourism with Silas Pemberton. "Just don't send any of your tourists up to the inn looking for Uncle Nicholas," she warned, "because if you do, I'll just have to tell them the truth about my uncle. That he never was a vampire."

With that, Hallie turned and stalked out the front door, swinging her new pail in one hand and her clam digger in the other. Damn Silas Pemberton and his de-

lusions of grandeur! The only thing she could hope for
was that his vampire festival was a complete and utter
failure.

Hallie started toward the inn, but her attention was
drawn to a small crowd that had gathered in front of the
town hall. As she approached, she could see her two
great-aunts, standing in the midst of the growing hub-
bub.

Hallie pushed her way through the group, which included all of Newton's vampire chapter and three or
four of the townsfolk.

"We found this next to your uncle Nicholas's grave,"
Newton said, his voice filled with excitement. He held
out a piece of cloth to the aunts and Prudence took it
from his hands. Patience bent over and examined it
carefully.

"It looks like a cravat," she said. "Wait! There seems
to be a monogram."

"N. R. T.," Newton said.

"Nicholas Redfield Tyler," Prudence said. "It must
be his."

Hallie stepped in and snatched the striped cravat
from her aunt's hand. "Where did you find this?" she
demanded.

"At your family plot," Newton said. "My group was
there searching for clues to the coming appearance of
your uncle and there it was, draped across the top of the
grave marker."

Hallie frowned and turned to her aunts. "What do
you know about this?" she asked.

They both blinked. "Why, nothing, dear," Patience
said uneasily.

"Although, I must say, this does appear to belong to Uncle Nick," Prudence continued. "In fact, I may even have a photograph of him wearing this very cravat."

"Could I see that photo?" Newton asked. "This could be exactly the proof we've been looking for!"

"Hold it right there!" Hallie cried. "Those photographs are family mementos and will not become part of this ridiculous search for a vampire."

"But this clue along with the approach of the new moon could be a valuable indicator," Newton whined. "I could print the photo in our newsletter."

Hallie glared at her aunts. "You two know better," she muttered. "We had a deal. Not another word about Uncle Nicholas."

Contrite expressions suffused their faces. "Perhaps we'd better return to our rehearsals, Sister," Patience said.

"Perhaps you're right," Prudence replied.

They both turned and scurried back inside the town hall. Gradually, the small group around Hallie dispersed, leaving her standing next to Newton. "I'd appreciate it if you'd keep this quiet," she said.

"But, Miss Tyler, I simply can't. This is much too important to our group. To the world."

"Mr. Knoblock, this cravat was not left in the graveyard by my uncle."

"Then how did it get there?"

Hallie sighed and stared down at the faded silk. "I don't know. But I'm going to find out and put an end to all this vampire business."

With that, she turned and headed back toward the inn. She tucked the cravat into her jacket pocket. Her jaw tightened as her fingers closed around the signet ring she'd found in the family graveyard two weeks ago. Someone was working awfully hard to perpetrate this vampire hoax.

A prickle of doubt skittered through her mind. But was it a hoax? Or was she simply so close-minded that she refused to see vampires no matter what proof she'd been shown. She'd spent so much energy denying the presence of the undead, perhaps she'd overlooked valid evidence.

Hallie stopped and shook her head, scolding herself inwardly. "I don't believe in vampires," she muttered.

But everyone else seemed to believe, including her aunts! Was she the only sane person left in Egg Harbor? Or was she just too stubborn to see the truth?

Hallie pulled the cravat from her pocket and looked down at it. She traced her finger over the embroidered monogram, then cursed softly. She felt as if she were trying to stop a runaway bus by hanging on to the back bumper.

No matter how much she wanted to deny it, maybe it was time to admit that there may just be some truth to all the legends.

"WHAT IS THAT SMELL?" Tris winced and held up his lantern, then stared across the wide flat of mud. "I thought New York City smelled bad, but it never smelled like this."

Hallie laughed, her green eyes reflecting the golden glow from the lantern. "That's what the ocean smells like at low tide. I think it smells kind of nice. Like it's alive."

Tris waved his hand in front of his face. "Only something very dead could smell this bad."

"You'll get used to it, city boy," Hallie teased. "Just breathe through your mouth."

Tris glanced over at her and their gazes locked. His breath caught in his throat and he had to tell himself to breathe again. Lord, she was beautiful, so achingly beautiful it hurt to think of ever being without her. He could spend a lifetime looking into that face, memorizing every detail and every nuance, and then memorizing them all over again.

"So, why did you bring me out here?" Tris asked softly, pulling his gaze away from hers. He stared down at the muck that sucked at the tall rubber boots Hallie had given him. He pulled his right foot out, only to have the left sink into the goop even further. "Certainly not for the romantic atmosphere."

"It's all part of digging clams," Hallie replied. "A New England tradition I think it's about time you experienced."

"That's why we're here? You made me crawl down all those rocks and wade through this muck for clams? Don't clams come in a can?"

"I have a craving for chowder and the only way to make a good clam chowder is with fresh clams. I promise you'll have fun."

Tris growled and shot her a narrow-eyed glare, bringing a smile to her face. "I slog through mud," he grumbled, "assailed by an overpowering odor, looking for something you can find in almost any grocery store. Now *that's* what I call fun. Maybe tomorrow I'll somersault down the bluff for a laugh."

Hallie slapped him playfully on the arm, then let her hand rest there, a gesture of such easy familiarity it caused a flood of warmth to seep through his limb. "Come on, Tris. I used to do this when I was a kid. It's easy." She handed him an oversize three-pronged fork with a long handle, then held up a shiny new bucket with his name painted on the side. "I've made you your very own clam bucket."

She held up the battered bucket she carried and by the light of her lantern, he made out the name Halimeda painted in big block letters.

"My dad gave me this when I was six," she said. "I used to come down here all the time. I discovered this clam flat. No one else knows the way down through the rocks but me."

He watched a gentle smile touch her lips at the memory. Tris held back a teasing reply, happy instead to listen to her soft, sweet voice relate a memory that was so obviously dear to her.

"I loved clamming," she continued. "My mother would come with us and sometimes we'd cook the clams right on the beach, just like the natives taught the pilgrims. My dad was a real history buff, so he liked having a clambake the old-fashioned way."

"He sounds like a nice man," Tris said, unable to keep a trace of envy out of his tone. He'd never been very close to his parents. They'd always been so busy, preferring to leave their painfully introverted son to his own devices. To tell the truth, he'd never really been close to anyone—until he'd met Hallie.

"He was," Hallie continued. "I'd help him dig a pit and line it with stones and then my father would build a fire of old driftwood inside the pit. We'd snuggle up next to the fire and get warm while my mother washed the clams. And then, when the fire was good and hot, we'd scrape the embers away and lay down a bed of damp seaweed on the hot rocks. Then my mother would put in the clams and potatoes and ears of corn still in their husks, and we'd cover it all with more seaweed and a big piece of leather and we'd wait."

Tris could picture a tiny version of Hallie, romping on the beach as her parents prepared a shore dinner. If he ever had a kid, he'd want that kid to grow up like Hallie did, with space to run and lots of fresh air. And with parents who really cared. And he'd want them to have a mother just like Hallie, a woman kind and patient and loving.

His mind lingered over the thought for a moment. He'd never really considered himself cut out for family life. But after nearly a month in Egg Harbor, in the peace and tranquility that surrounded the tiny seacoast town, he could almost imagine a different life for himself. A life that included Hallie.

Tris cursed silently. Hell, he hadn't even told Hallie who he really was. Why was he waiting? The longer he procrastinated, the more difficult it would be. Maybe it was because he represented everything she'd been fighting against in Egg Harbor.

He was a celebrity. And with his fame came fans and photographers and the kind of attention that Hallie had never wanted. Celebrity relationships were almost doomed from the start, especially if one half of the relationship didn't share the spotlight.

Could he really expect Hallie to cheerfully accept all the difficulties that came along as part of his life? He cared about her. To be truthful, he was falling in love with her and he didn't want her to suffer because of his choices in life. What he wouldn't give to remain anonymous, to remain Edward Tristan.

Tris pushed his doubts aside and smiled down at Hallie. He bent over and poked at the muck with the fork. "So, are these clams sleeping?"

"No," Hallie said with a laugh.

"Then do we have to sneak up on them in the dark and poke them with this fork?"

She rolled her eyes and shook her head.

Tris frowned. "Then why are we out here in the middle of the cold, damp night?"

"Because it's low tide and I'm too busy during the day to come out here. Besides, you're the one who stays up all night. Come on, let's go." Tris watched as she began to plod through the muck toward the water.

"Where are you going?" he called.

"They're out here," she said, pointing toward the receding waterline. "Beneath where fifteen feet of water used to be."

Tris grudgingly followed her, swinging the bucket at his side and admiring the gentle sway of her hips by lantern light. He'd walked out nearly fifty feet when Hallie stopped and squatted. "This is what you're looking for," she said, holding the lantern close to the muck. "They're like little bubbles. Dimples," she said, shoving her fork into the smooth muck. She pushed down on the handle of the fork and, much to Tris's amazement, a small clam popped out of the mud. She brushed the goop off and handed it to him. "These are long-necked clams. They have softer shells. Put it in your bucket. Then hold the lantern close to the sand and look for the dimples."

Tris watched as Hallie bent to survey the mud flat. She looked so pretty, her hair blowing in the stiff breeze, her expression intense but incredibly guileless.

He'd always thought small-town life would be dull. But Hallie found something interesting for them to do every time they were together. One night they had hiked up to an old lighthouse that stood high on a bluff above the harbor. Another night, she took him down to the dock and they watched as the lobster fishermen mended their traps. She lived a simple and unpretentious life, a life he'd come to envy. A life he could see stretching into the future, the two of them together, happy and content.

For the next hour Tris walked beside Hallie, digging up clams and dropping them in his bucket. When both of their buckets were full, they walked back along the base of the bluff on the tiny strip of sand until they found the spot where they'd come down.

Tris picked up a piece of driftwood. He didn't want the night to end. Hallie had been right, he'd had fun digging for clams. "Let's build a fire," he said.

Hallie turned to him and smiled. "That would be nice. We've still got a few hours before the tide starts back in."

"A few hours?" Tris asked.

"When the tide comes back in, this beach all but disappears under water. It's quite dangerous to be caught out here. But we'll have time." She patted her jacket pockets then reached inside and pulled out a book of matches. "Why don't you look for some big pieces of wood and I'll look for kindling. It's best to stick close to the bluff. The wood there is usually drier."

They gathered plenty of wood, then set the lanterns in the sand and lit the fire. Fifteen minutes later, it blazed nearly four feet high in the air, sending a shower of sparks into the inky black sky.

Tris sat down next to Hallie and put his arm around her shoulders, pulling her close. "This is perfect," he said.

Hallie stared into the fire. "Mmm," she said. "It is, isn't it."

Tris turned and looked at her, her lovely features illuminated by the light from the fire. He reached out, turned her gaze toward his, then bent his head and kissed her. He thought a simple kiss would be enough, but in the perfect instant when her lips touched his, he couldn't help but want more.

He was falling in love with Hallie, an emotion he'd never experienced before. Tris wrapped his arms around her waist and pulled her down on top of him, fitting her body against his, needing to touch every soft curve.

He'd always kept such a tight leash on his desire, knowing that Hallie preferred to take things slowly between them. But his feelings had changed and along with the realization that he was falling in love with her came the need to possess her.

He waited for Hallie to stiffen beneath his touch, knowing that it would signal the end of his passion, but as he skimmed his hands along her body, she pressed herself more tightly against him.

Her hands moved to the front of his coat and she tugged it back and worked at the buttons of his shirt. Slowly, she nuzzled his chest, working her way down with each button she undid.

Tris moaned softly as her tongue traced a line from his collarbone to his nipple. He pressed his hips against hers, the ridge of his desire growing harder with every breath. He wanted to take her then and there, on the sand, by the light of the fire.

But he couldn't. Not now. When he made love to her, he wanted nothing standing between them. No lies, no deceit, nothing that might put their future in jeopardy.

Tris furrowed his fingers through her hair. "Hallie," he said softly.

She looked up at him and smiled, her eyes hazy with passion.

"Hallie, there's something I have to tell you."

A slight frown marred her forehead. "Am I doing something wrong?"

Tris shook his head. "No, not at all. It's just that . . ." He paused, then cursed his own indecision. The truth should make no difference at all. But what if it did? What if it sent her running? Could he take that chance?

He let out a tightly held breath. "Maybe we'd better go up," he said.

She blinked. "Do you want to go back?" she asked, her voice breathless with surprise.

"Hallie, sweetheart, it's a little dangerous on this beach, and not because of the tide. If we don't go up now, I'm going to make love to you right here on the sand. Is that what you want to happen?"

She rolled off him and sat up, clearly not ready to deal with that prospect. "I'm sorry," she said, brushing the sand off her knees.

Tris groaned inwardly. "You don't have to be sorry."

She scrambled to her feet and grabbed her bucket. Good God, how was he expected to keep his resolve around this woman? Every time she touched him, all he could think about was losing himself inside her.

Tris pushed himself to his feet and caught her hand as she turned. "Hallie, I—"

"You're right. We better go," she murmured as she hurried toward the base of the bluff.

They picked their way back up the bluff, following the narrow, winding path through the huge granite boulders. Tris followed Hallie, keeping a protective hand on her back as she nimbly climbed, her clam bucket and fork grasped in one hand.

But when they reached the top of the bluff, she picked up her pace, murmuring only a quick good-night to him before she grabbed his bucket and slipped through the back door of the inn.

Tris sighed and ran his fingers through his hair, then tipped his head back. What the hell was wrong with him? He couldn't make love to her until she knew the truth about him. Yet he couldn't tell her the truth for fear she wouldn't make love to him.

"Damned if I do and damned if I don't," Tris said softly.

HALLIE STOOD at her bedroom window staring out into the darkness. Through the thick woods, a single light was visible from the coach house, a light that held her transfixed. She fingered the garnet cross that hung around her neck, sliding it back and forth against the chain.

An undeniable power drew her thoughts toward that light, toward the man who waited for her there. In her mind she could hear him speak to her soul.

You will come to me, Hallie. You can't resist.

It was as if he could reach inside her mind and control her passion. He knew her deepest fantasies and he challenged her with every touch to allow those fantasies to take flight. She closed her eyes, yet his image remained burned in her brain, pulsing with a power that both frightened and intrigued her. She wanted to resist, yet with every heartbeat she felt herself drawn toward him against her will.

You can't resist me, Hallie.

She stepped away from the window and walked toward the bed. But she knew she'd never be able to fall asleep. He'd haunt her dreams until her body ached with unfulfilled desire.

Hallie pulled a shawl from the bedstead and wrapped it tightly around her, trying to quell the trembling that had taken hold of her body. She wandered out of her bedroom to the front parlor of the inn and stood in front of the dying embers of a fire. The clocked ticked softly on the mantel, the sound matching the drum of her pulse.

The fire offered no warmth, no safety from the voice in her head and no remedy for the ache inside her. She wandered into the tiny library just off the parlor and turned on the lamp, then distractedly scanned the shelves for a book to read. Resting on the library table was one of Newton's vampire volumes.

She picked it up and flipped through the pages, then closed her eyes. If she had a single doubt in her mind about Edward Tristan, she would never consider going to him. Yet, she couldn't deny the unnatural power he held over her, a power no man had ever held over her.

Hallie slammed the book shut in frustration, then padded to the front door. But did that mean he wasn't human? She pulled it open and drew a deep breath of the night air, hoping it would clear her senses, but the same thought remained embedded in her mind. She wanted him. No matter how hard she tried to deny her feelings, she wanted Tris.

Hesitantly, she took a step outside, her bare foot warm against the cold wood of the porch. She took another step. And then another. Moments later, she found herself standing at the bottom of the porch steps. And then she ran, across the lawn and toward the woods.

The branches caught on her shawl as she stumbled down the narrow path to the coach house. The light. She had to get to the light. He would be there and he would be able to quell this ache inside of her.

And then she stood at the door. She hesitated for a moment, then slowly removed the cross from around her neck and tucked it into the pocket of her nightgown. Then she reached out and turned the knob, pushing the door open. The brisk wind whipped her nightgown around her bare legs and she pulled the shawl more tightly around her.

He sat bent over the desk, scribbling on a pad of paper. She watched him for a long time. Slowly he became aware of her presence, of the cold draft that skimmed through the room. He turned around and stared at her, then pushed himself out of his chair and strode to the door.

"I—I'm not sure why I'm here," she said, breathless, her gaze fixed on his.

He reached out and pulled her inside the coach house, then softly closed the door behind her. "You're cold," he said, rubbing her arms with his palms. He glanced down at her feet. "Jesus, Hallie, you're not wearing any shoes!"

"I—I had to come," she said. "But I wasn't sure if I should."

"What's wrong?"

"You don't know what it's been like. I had to know, but I didn't want to know."

"What? What do you want to know?"

She crossed her arms in front of her and tried to rub away the goose bumps that grew beneath his intense gaze. "I'm not sure . . . who you are. Sometimes I think I know you, but then other times, you're like a stranger to me."

A wary look crossed his face. "Who do you think I am, Hallie?" he asked.

She bit her bottom lip and fought the urge to flee. But he held her and she was unable to move, unable to ignore the desire that seemed to well up inside of her. "My aunts think you're a—" She paused, unable to bring herself to say the word.

Vampire. Patience and Prudence believed him to be a vampire.

"Newton thinks you are, too. I tried not to believe them, but they had all this proof."

He closed his eyes and pulled her toward him, wrapping his arms around her trembling body. "God, Hallie, I wanted to tell you, but I thought it might ruin everything between us. I should have told you at the very start. I was wrong to hide it from you."

She pushed herself back and gazed up at him, her eyes wide. "Then you are . . ."

He kissed her temple. "I never meant to hurt you. And I never will. I swear to God. If I could change who I was, I would. For you. I love you, Hallie."

Hallie's breath caught in her throat at his words.

"Tell me it doesn't make a difference," he said. "Tell me it's all right."

She wanted to run, to flee as fast as she could, for she knew she'd never be able to resist him. But she couldn't make herself move, couldn't pull herself from his touch. He had taken hold of her soul and she was no longer in control.

"And I love you, Tris," she said in a quiet voice, unable to stop the words any more than she could stop her need for him.

He looked down at her, a smile of relief curling the corners of his mouth. Hallie felt a familiar tug on her senses, an overwhelming magnetism that seemed to dissolve the last shred of self-preservation she possessed.

Tris slipped his hands around her waist and brushed his mouth against hers in an undemanding kiss. But slowly, as he teased at her mouth with his tongue, his kiss became more urgent, more demanding.

"Why did you come here, Hallie?" he murmured against the curve of her neck.

"I—I had to come," Hallie said, letting her shawl drop to the floor. "I couldn't stay away any longer."

She cupped his face in her hands and brought his mouth back to hers, kissing him as he had kissed her, with total abandon and complete possession. She stretched herself fully against him, molding her body to his, a desperate need growing inside her.

He moaned softly and clutched her buttocks in his hands, pressing her hips into his, rubbing his growing desire against her stomach. Every nerve in her body cried out for his touch and she strained to eliminate the space between them, trying to make hard muscle and soft flesh become one through the soft flannel of her nightgown and the denim of his jeans.

Tris's breath quickened and he tugged at her nightgown, pulling it up along her hips, skimming his palms along her legs. She wanted to be rid of her clothes, wanted to feel his body against her bare skin, and she broke their kiss for an instant to pull her nightgown over her head and throw it to the floor.

She stood naked before him, watching his gaze as it took in her body, unafraid, yet completely aware of her power over him.

"You're beautiful," he murmured, reaching out to cup her breast in his warm palm. He slowly teased at her nipple with his thumb, bringing it to a hard peak that sent shivers coursing through her body.

Hallie drew a deep breath and her teeth chattered. He gently took her hand and led her toward the fireplace where a fire burned brightly, throwing off a delicious heat that warmed her skin. Slowly, without ever taking his gaze from hers, he undressed until he, too, stood naked in front of her.

Her eyes drifted down the length of him, lingering on the proof of his need for her. And then she knew that she wanted him. She wanted his hard mouth covering hers, his lean body pressed against hers. She wanted to knead the muscles of his broad back with her fingers while he moved inside her. A wave of desire passed through her, sending a rush of moisture to the core of her passion.

She stepped into his arms and furrowed her hands through his long hair. Her nipples grazed the soft sprinkling of hair on his chest and his mouth found hers again. Their hands frantically explored each other's bodies until Hallie pulled back, knowing they would never be close enough until he was inside her.

"Make love to me, Tris. Please," she murmured.

In one smooth motion, he picked her up into his arms and carried her to the bedroom, then placed her gently on the bed. He stared down at her, his feverish eyes studying her intensely, taking in every inch of her body. Then he laid down beside her and pulled her against him, sliding his leg over her hip possessively.

His kiss was urgent and uncontrolled, his mouth ravaging hers until she could barely draw a breath, his lips skimming across her face and her chest. His hands danced over her body, searching out the spots that set her senses on fire.

Hallie moaned in pleasure. She felt alive, more alive than she had in years. Free of her inhibitions and apprehensions about the choices she'd made. And free to be as wild and wanton as Tris's needs demanded. She abandoned herself to his touch, allowing her nerves to sing with excitement and desire, and giving over to the need to return that pleasure to him.

Hallie let her hands drift down Tris's back, splaying her fingers over his narrow hips. Then she tentatively wrapped her fingers around the hard ridge of his arousal, wondering at the blazing heat and satin feel of him.

Tris sucked in his breath and grabbed Hallie's wrist to still her movements. "Ah, sweetheart, don't do that. If you touch me like that, things will be over before they even begin."

He gave her a gentle kiss and pulled her on top of him, slowing the headlong pace of their passion. With deliberate movements, he positioned her thighs alongside his until she straddled his waist and his heat rested along the crease of her moist desire.

Hallie moved against him, positioning herself over his probing tip then sliding back along the hot, hard ridge. His eyes were closed and his jaw was clenched and Hallie watched him deny the pleasure she was so close to giving him. It had been so long since she had made love with a man. She had forgotten the incredible feelings, the waves of sensation, the humming nerves and tensed muscles.

"Make love to me, Tris," she murmured, her body tensed and ready for release. She wanted him. Not just his body, but his soul, his being, his love. She wanted him to become part of her.

Tris turned slightly and stretched to grab his shaving kit from the bedside table, then withdrew a small packet. He handed it to her. "Soon, Hallie. Just take care of this for me, sweetheart."

With sure fingers, she sheathed him. And this time when she felt him probe at her entrance, she didn't pull away, but pushed herself slowly down on top of him, burying him deep within her.

Tris's eyes locked with hers and she watched an expression of pure pleasure suffuse his face. He opened his mouth to say something, but she had already begun to move above him, and his words turned to a soft moan.

Faster and faster they moved, Tris thrusting up to meet her body. She felt a tiny knot of tension deep in her core twist and tingle with his every movement, begging for release. When his fingers slid between their bodies to massage the nub of her passion, she felt herself hurtling toward the edge.

She gave herself over to the delicious feeling, releasing her fears along with her control, focusing purely on his touch. She was his and his alone. He possessed her like no man had ever done before, and no man could ever do after.

Wave after wave of glorious sensation washed over her. Through her haze, she heard Tris groan as he reached his climax with her, driving into her with shudders and spasms.

Spiraling downward, her breath coming in ragged gasps, Hallie collapsed on top of him. Her lips brushed along his shoulder and she could taste the saltiness of his sweaty skin. She stayed absolutely still, not wanting to break their intimate connection. Slowly, her heartbeat regained its regular rhythm and her breathing calmed. She wanted to speak, but instead, buried her face in the curve of his neck and closed her eyes.

There would be time for words later, time to face their lives beyond the walls of the coach house. But for now, she simply wanted to fall asleep in his arms, knowing that when desire haunted her dreams she need only open her eyes and reach for him.

8

THE SUN had barely lifted above the horizon when Hallie opened her eyes. She snuggled down beneath the covers, pulling them up to her nose and hoping to catch just a few minutes more sleep before she had to get up and start breakfast for her guests.

As her mind began to clear, she mentally went through the morning's menu, adding up the time it would take to prepare the dishes she had planned. Laundry was the next item on the agenda. But something else niggled at her mind and she pinched her eyes shut, trying to recall whether she'd forgotten to buy an ingredient or prepare a guest room.

Slowly, realization dawned and she opened her eyes to find herself not in her own bedroom in the inn, but in the bedroom of the coach house. Hallie gasped, then sat up in bed, yanking the covers up with her. She glanced beneath the sheets, then groaned.

"I'm naked," she murmured.

She turned to look at the other side of the bed, then breathed a sigh of relief when she found it empty. She pinched her eyes shut again, then opened them. Suddenly the events of the previous night came flooding back to her mind with unsettling clarity.

She remembered her dreams and her restlessness, the overpowering urge to go to Tris, to find him and to give in to the need that coursed through her body. She remembered stepping out onto the front porch of the inn and then running through the woods.

But the rest . . . the rest was just a hazy melange of desperate longing and arousing sensation. They'd made love last night, of that much she was sure. And it had been more amazing than she'd ever imagined it could be. Tris had taken her to a place she'd never been before, showing her the heights of desire and the sheer limits of passion.

She turned over onto her side and hesitantly reached out to run her palm along the cool sheets. She made love to him last night, but where was he now? She frowned. Perhaps he'd thought it better to let her wake up alone so she could deal with what had happened the night before. Perhaps she was supposed to get dressed now. Or perhaps—

Her breath stopped in her throat and she clapped her hand to her neck. Her gaze skipped to the window and she blinked against the light.

"Sunrise," she murmured.

The sun had come up and Tris was gone, his side of the bed cold. Hallie softly called his name, then shouted it out, but there was no answer, only a smothering silence that stole the breath from her body.

Hurriedly, Hallie kicked off the covers and searched the room for something to wear. She found one of Tris's shirts and tugged it on, then raced out of the bedroom to the bathroom. She flipped on the light and stared at herself in the mirror.

"Calm down," she said to herself. "There's nothing to be afraid of." She took a deep breath and pulled her hand from her neck. Tipping her head to the side, she searched for the telltale teeth marks. But her neck was smooth and unblemished. She released her tightly held breath, then checked the other side of her neck. She saw nothing to indicate that she'd been— She cursed softly. "Bitten," she said out loud.

Relief surged through her, followed by utter embarrassment. Hallie stared at her reflection and shook her head. "You thought you'd been bitten? Good Lord, Hallie Tyler, all this vampire business has addled your brain!"

But just as the events of the previous night came back to her, so did snippets of conversation. She'd asked him . . . and he'd told her. The rumors about him were true. He had admitted it. But he also promised that he would never hurt her. She looked at her neck again. He'd kept that promise, for now.

But was she really supposed to believe he was a vampire? Every instinct told her that it wasn't true. She didn't believe in vampires. Yet all the evidence pointed in that direction. She pressed the heels of her hands to her temples.

So what if he was a vampire? What would she do? She tried to marshal her jumbled thoughts and think objectively about the possibility.

First of all, she'd have to seriously revise her beliefs. It would be hard to live with a vampire and at the same time refuse to acknowledge his existence. And there was his rather unusual diet. What did one serve a vampire for dinner? Then, there was the future to be considered. When she turned eighty, Tris would still be as young as the day she'd met him.

"I'd be the envy of every woman at the senior center," she said to herself as she paced the length of the bathroom. "Including Prissy Pemberton."

Hallie shook her head. Coming to terms with Tris's immortality was going to be much harder than she'd ever imagined, more so since she still couldn't believe he might be immortal.

She walked out of the bathroom and stood in the middle of the great room, not certain what she should do. But her curiosity got the better of her and she slowly began to examine his personal belongings, looking for clues to the man she'd made love to. She ran her hands over the fabric of his coat, which was tossed over the back of the sofa. She opened a laptop computer she found on the coffee table. And she picked up his clothes, scattered in front of the fireplace where he'd left them.

As she grabbed his jeans, his wallet fell out of the back pocket. She snatched it up and hastily put it back inside the pocket. But then, a few moments later, she glanced around the empty house and pulled it out again.

The picture from his New York driver's license stared back at her as she opened it and she examined it more closely. His birthdate put him at thirty-six years old. Her gaze drifted to the name on the license and she blinked in confusion. "Edward Tristan Montgomery," she murmured. "Montgomery?"

Why did the name sound so familiar? And why had Tris registered under his first and middle name? "Edward T. Montgomery," she said, trying to recall where she'd heard the name before.

She distractedly put the wallet back in his pocket and laid his jeans over the back of the sofa. Then she collected her own clothes, while the name ran through her head over and over again. Where had she heard it before?

Hallie slipped out of Tris's shirt and pulled on her nightgown, then wrapped her shawl around her shoulders. She didn't have time to think about this now. She had to get back to the inn before her aunts woke up. She'd figure this all out later, after Tris—woke up.

Hallie headed for the door, then stopped, still unable to forget her suspicions. If she truly wanted to know the truth about Tris, she had the means. If he was a vampire, he was here, somewhere in this house, hiding from the daylight. She closed her eyes and drew a deep breath, then walked across the great room to the cellar door. Vampires usually kept their coffins in the cellar, didn't they?

"You've been in this cellar hundreds of times," she told herself. "There's nothing to be afraid of." She took the stairs slowly, but when Hallie reached the bottom, she found the dank and musty cellar empty.

She quickly climbed the stairs and slammed the cellar door behind her. If the coffin wasn't in the basement, where was it? She glanced around the room and her gaze stopped at the door to the spare bedroom. "All right," she murmured. "Just open the door. If it's in there, you'll have to deal with it sometime."

She slowly turned the knob, but what met her gaze was more troubling than she'd ever anticipated. The coffin was there, in the center of the room. All the drapes had been drawn and the room was eerily dark and silent. She took a step toward the coffin, then hesitated. If he was inside, she really didn't want to know, did she?

But she couldn't help herself. She *had* to know. She had to have that one irrefutable piece of proof that he was what she suspected him to be. With hesitant steps, she approached the coffin. She held out her hand and touched the cool, smooth wood, then yanked it away.

"Do it, Hallie," she murmured. "Open it. You want to know for sure. Here's your chance."

Taking a fortifying breath, she reached down and slowly lifted the lid. Inch by inch, it came up, but she was afraid to look inside. She stared straight ahead, her eyes fixed on the far side of the room, her heart pounding so hard she thought it might burst.

"Hallie?"

The sound of his voice shot right to her heart and she jumped and let out a piercing scream! The coffin lid slipped from her hand and slammed down on the fingers of her other hand. She snatched her arm back and pressed her bruised fingers between her legs, hopping up and down to quell the waves of pain. Her heart felt as if it had leapt into her throat and threatened to strangle her.

"Hallie? What's wrong?"

A hand touched her shoulder and she screamed again, then spun around and swung her elbow out, grazing Tris's jaw. His head snapped back and he looked at her in shock. Hallie covered her mouth with her hand and stared up at him, wide-eyed and trembling.

"Damn it, Hallie, what's going on?"

With a shaking hand, she reached out and touched him, patting her palm along his chest. "You're...you're here."

"Of course, I'm here. Where else would I be?"

She glanced over her shoulder at the coffin, then back at him. "But you weren't here when I woke up. I thought you were . . . gone."

He smiled crookedly and rubbed his sore jaw. "I walked down to the bakery to pick up some breakfast. I thought we might have coffee together before you had to go back to the inn."

Her eyes widened and her breath caught in her chest. "You want me to have breakfast with you?"

He nodded. "Is that so strange? I'm hungry."

Hallie swallowed hard and tried to still her spinning thoughts. "Could you come with me?" she asked, motioning him out of the bedroom. Tris followed her back into the great room. "Would you stand over there?" she said, pointing to a spill of sunlight shining through the coach house window. He did as he was told and Hallie held her breath, expecting him to disappear in a puff of smoke. But he didn't.

"Can we eat now?" he finally asked, a frown wrinkling his brow.

Hallie shook her head, confusion scattering her thoughts like leaves in the wind. "I—I can't. I have to get back to the inn before I'm missed. The aunts will be up and they'll wonder where I am."

He crossed the room and took her hands in his, then gazed down into her eyes. "Are you sure you're all right, Hallie? You seem upset. You don't regret what happened last night, do you?"

She shook her head. "I'm fine. I'm just fine. No regrets. None at all."

He bent and tugged a pair of his shoes on her bare feet, then brushed a soft kiss on her lips. "I guess I'll have to let you go. But you have to promise to come back as soon as you can." He kissed her again, this time more deeply. "We have a lot to talk about. Do you promise?"

She forced a smile. "As soon as I can," she said before hurrying through the door. Stumbling up the path in his too large shoes, she glanced back at the coach house once and frowned, then stopped in the middle of the path, gulping in a long breath of the cool morning air.

"Get a hold of yourself, Hallie. You can figure this out." She pulled her shawl tightly around her shoulders and started toward the inn again. "He wasn't sleeping in the coffin, he eats breakfast and he's able to stand in sunlight." She tipped her head back and groaned. "I'm so confused!"

She thought she'd known the man she'd made love to, the man she was falling in love with. But after what had just transpired, Hallie wondered if she really knew him at all.

HALLIE BALANCED a pitcher of freshly squeezed orange juice on a tray already loaded with glasses, then pushed through the swinging door from the kitchen to the dining room. She yawned, then blinked hard, trying to stay awake for just a little bit longer.

The dining room was full, twenty-one guests all ready for their complimentary breakfast at the exact same time. Prudence and Patience had set baskets of fresh muffins on the tables and were now assembling eggs Benedict atop warmed plates in the kitchen.

To Hallie's great relief, she'd made it back to the inn before the aunts had risen, but her night with Tris and her very confusing morning had put her woefully behind schedule and well depleted of energy.

"Miss Tyler! Oh, Miss Tyler!"

Hallie groaned inwardly at the sound of Newton Knoblock's whiny greeting. She'd wondered just how long Tris would stay in Egg Harbor and she'd was beginning to wonder the same of Newton Knoblock. Didn't the man have a life? He'd been here for almost a month and showed no signs of leaving.

"Good morning, Mr. Knoblock," she said as she placed a glass of orange juice in front of him.

"Good morning, Hallie. How did you sleep last night?"

Hallie swallowed hard, then smiled, her mind flashing back to her evening with Tris. "I—I slept fine." Better than fine. She hadn't slept so well since before Tris arrived at the inn. "And you, Mr. Knoblock? How did you sleep?"

He shoved his glasses up onto the bridge of his nose and shook his head. "Not well. That mattress in my room really should be turned on a regular basis. It's become very lumpy. And the heating system in this house needs to be fixed. The temperature in my room was too high to allow a good night's sleep."

Hallie nodded. "I'll look into that, Mr. Knoblock. By the way, I was wondering when you would be leaving. I've had a lot of requests for reservations for the next few weeks and I'd really like to get my bookings settled."

"I'm not sure," he said. "I feel that my work here has just begun."

She ground her teeth. "Don't you have a job, Newton?"

He sniffled, then shook his head. "I don't need one. I'm independently wealthy. My father made millions in plastics."

"You're independently wealthy?"

He nodded. "You know those plastic vampire teeth. Knoblock Industries. Fifty million sets a year at a cost of just pennies. They retail for a dollar. Around Halloween, two dollars."

Hallie chuckled in disbelief. "Is that why you founded Undead International?" she asked.

"It only makes sense," he replied. "It's call synergy. All the business experts are talking about it." He took a long drink of his orange juice, then placed his glass neatly beside his plate. Hallie picked up her tray and prepared to move on to the next table, but his voice stopped her.

"Oh, Miss Tyler," Newton called, "I meant to tell you. I remembered where I've seen Mr. Tristan before."

Hallie spun around and returned to his side. "Mr. Tristan? My— I mean, our Mr. Tristan?"

He nodded. "Actually, it's not Mr. *Tristan*. It's Mr. Montgomery. Tristan Montgomery."

"Edward Tristan Montgomery?"

Newton shook his head. "No. Just Tristan Montgomery. No Edward."

Hallie sighed impatiently. "So where do you know him from?"

"Well, I don't actually know him. I've just seen him. His picture. On the backs of his books."

Hallie's heart stopped for an instant. "What books?"

"Mr. Tristan is really Tristan Montgomery, the horror novelist. I can't believe I didn't recognize him. He's quite a celebrity. I've read all his books and seen him on television any number of times. I can't believe I didn't recognize him. But then, my mind has been occupied elsewhere."

Hallie set her tray down on the table with a thud. "He's a celebrity?"

"*New York Times*'s bestselling author," Newton informed her. "Millions of copies of his books are in print. And he's quite the ladies' man if I remember correctly."

Hallie's jaw tightened. "Mr. Knoblock, would you be kind enough to pass around the orange juice? I believe I have some business to discuss with Mr. Tristan."

"Mr. Montgomery," Newton corrected. "I told you to watch out for him. Didn't I say that? The man is dangerous."

Hallie raced through the dining room into the kitchen, then murmured a few quick orders to Prudence and Patience before she stormed out the back door.

How could he? After all the time they'd spent together, he never once mentioned his career—or his status as a rather well-known novelist. No wonder she recognized his name. After all, she did consider herself rather widely read and though she'd never picked up one of his books, she'd seen them in bookstores.

Her temper grew with each step she took. Didn't she have a right to know? After all, they were lovers and lovers were supposed to be honest with each other. For all she knew, he could be married with three kids and a dog, as well!

She hurried up the path to the coach house then pounded on the door. Her summons was met with an almost immediate response. Tris swung the door open and smiled when he saw her. But his smile quickly faded at her angry expression.

She stalked inside, then turned back to him, her fury barely under control. "How could you?" Hallie demanded, her fists clenched.

Tris frowned. "How could I what?"

"How could you lie to me? How could you make love to me and not tell me who you really were? What else don't I know about you?"

Tris blinked hard and shook his head. "What are you talking about? You knew who I was."

"I knew that you were Tristan Montgomery? I *didn't* know, because you didn't tell me."

Tris raked his hands through his hair. "But you *said* you knew," he countered.

She braced her hands on her hips and stomped her foot angrily. "I said nothing of the kind," she replied. "I didn't know until this morning. Newton told me at breakfast. He said he recognized you from the back of one of your books. He told me you're a very famous writer. I made love to a very famous writer and I didn't even know."

Tris sighed. "Hallie, I thought you knew. Last night you—"

"Last night I thought you were a vampire!" she said. "Not a damned celebrity. A vampire! That's different."

Tris gasped and stared at her in disbelief. "You came here last night and made love with me, all the while believing I was a vampire?" He cursed softly. "Good God, Hallie, what were you thinking? How could you believe I was a vampire? And how could you make love to a man you suspected was a vampire?"

She glared at him as she paced back and forth across the great room. "How am I supposed to feel about this? Should I be glad that you're not Edward Tristan? I fell in love with Edward Tristan, not Tristan Montgomery. And I thought Edward Tristan was a vampire!"

Tris raked his fingers through his hair and studied her for a long moment. "Let me get this straight. You fell in love with a vampire. I just happen to be a successful working novelist—a man who is very much alive, I might add—but you'd rather have the vampire?"

"What about the coffin?" she demanded. "And sleeping all day? And you never eat!"

"The coffin was a joke," he explained. "My agent sent it after she found out I was working on a new vampire story. And I always work at night. As for meals, I eat all the time. Just ask Earl down at the diner. He's been feeding me for weeks."

Hallie stopped her pacing. "Why did you come here?"

Tris laughed and shook his head. "Would you believe for some peace and quiet? But after I arrived, I learned about the vampire legend and it gave me a good idea for my newest book. I decided to stay and soak up the atmosphere."

Hallie squeezed her eyes shut. "You know how I feel about this town. You know how important it is to me. And yet, you used us all. We took you in and all the time you were watching us, looking for something to put in your damn book."

"That's not true, Hallie. I haven't done anything to you or this town."

"Yes, you have," she said, tipping her chin up stubbornly. "You lied to me. You're not the man I thought you were."

"I'm exactly the man you made love to, Hallie. I wasn't lying then."

She met his gaze defiantly. "I want you to leave. Today. Get your things together and go."

Tris crossed the room in three long steps, then grabbed her arms and gave her a gentle shake. "Don't do this, Hallie," he warned. "Don't use this as an excuse to run away from me again. I know this scares you, but you can't stop loving me. And I know you love me. You said you did and you can't take that back."

"I loved Edward Tristan. I don't even know you," she responded.

"I'm the same man, Hallie. Look at me. I haven't changed." He placed his palm over his heart. "What's in here hasn't changed."

She pulled out of his grasp and crossed her arms beneath her breasts. "What did you think it would do to this town when everyone learned who you were?"

"Hallie, I'm not that famous."

"The Vampire Festival and the great novelist, Tristan Montgomery, all in one place? And a new book about vampires in Egg Harbor! The mayor will welcome you and all your famous friends with open arms. Maybe you planned this all along. It makes for great publicity, don't you think?"

"I don't give a damn about publicity," Tris retorted. "And I don't have any famous friends. The truth be told, I don't have any friends at all. You're the first person I've allowed into my life for years and I'm not going to let you go."

Hallie took a deep breath and shook her head. "I want you out of here and out of Egg Harbor. You can settle your bill and leave." She paused. "In fact, don't even bother. I don't want your money. Just go. Get out of my life."

With that, Hallie spun on her heel and rushed out of the coach house, tears pushing at the corners of her eyes. "I won't cry," she said to herself as she hurried back down the path to the inn. "I never loved him. I don't need him. And I won't cry. I won't cry."

She shoved the back door open and hurried through the kitchen, passing her aunts without a word. When she'd reached the safety of her own room, she slammed the door behind her and locked it, then laid down on the bed and curled herself into a tiny ball.

She fought the tears as hard as she'd ever fought anything in her life, refusing to acknowledge that he was worth it. She didn't love him. And if she didn't love him, then it wouldn't hurt to lose him. Not like it had hurt when she lost her parents. No, she would never hurt like that again, because she wouldn't allow it!

Edward Tristan, or Tristan Montgomery, or whoever he was, was out of her life for good now. And she was safe.

HALLIE SAT on a large rock, her knees tucked beneath her chin and her gaze fixed on the ocean. The crisp autumn breeze fluttered through her hair and chilled her cheeks and ears, but she didn't want to go back inside. Out here, she could breathe. Inside, she felt as if she might suffocate.

She glanced over her shoulder at the inn, then looked back at the water. Years ago, the Tyler women used to stand on the widow's walk, watching for their husbands to return from their long sea voyages. It was easy to understand how they felt, the emptiness of their days, the loneliness of the nights.

Since Tris had left, she'd felt the same way, as if a part of her heart had been wrenched away against her will. Only he'd never return. She would watch and wait for him, but he was gone for good. She had seen to that.

She took another breath of the tangy air. For the past three days she'd had to put up with her aunts fussing and fretting. They had watched her every move as if she were hovering on the edge of a breakdown. And no matter how many times she assured them she was all right, they refused to believe her.

She *was* all right. Tris was out of her life and now everything could get back to normal. She could focus on the inn and her work. And after the rush of guests died down, she could use the profits she'd made to complete the coach house.

A dull ache twisted at her heart. She used to dream of making the coach house her home. But now, she wasn't sure she'd ever be able to walk in the door without thinking of Tris. He'd become a part of that house, like the furniture and the fireplace. When she walked in the door, she expected to see him, dressed in black, his hair rumpled.

Why had she ordered him to leave? Because he had lied to her! He'd neglected to tell her who he really was.

She sighed. Was that the real reason, or simply her own rationalization? Had he been right when he said she was afraid of what was happening between them?

He left. Whether she pushed him out or he departed of his own free will, deep inside, she knew he'd have to leave sometime. He was a famous writer. He didn't belong in Egg Harbor any more than . . .

She bit her bottom lip. "Any more than Jonathan did," she murmured.

Jonathan had claimed to love her, but he'd deserted her when she needed him most. In fact, everyone she'd ever loved had left her. Her parents, Jonathan, they'd all gone, leaving her to live life on her own.

But Tris was not Jonathan. She'd never felt about her ex-fiancé the way she felt about Tris, so full of passion and life. When she thought about her future with Tris, she imagined wonderful possibilities. A perfect life in Egg Harbor, children, a happy home. And a love that would last for years and years.

"Miss Tyler?"

Hallie closed her eyes at the sound of Newton's voice. She didn't need his company, especially now. But he was a guest, and Hallie was always cordial to guests.

She turned and forced a smile. "Hello, Mr. Knoblock. What can I do for you?"

"Actually, I thought I might do something for you," Newton said hesitantly. "Here. I thought you might be interested in this." He held out a book and Hallie hesitated. She didn't need any more information on vampires. She'd had quite enough of the whole subject. But she took the book anyway.

"It's one of Tristan Montgomery's novels," Newton explained. "I thought you might enjoy reading it. After all, he is a guest here. Probably the most famous guest ever to visit the Widow's Walk."

"Mr. Montgomery checked out a few days ago," Hallie said softly. "He had to get back to New York."

Newton frowned. "But I just saw him this morning."

Hallie sat up straight and shook her head. "That can't be."

"Oh, but it is. He was walking down Main Street. I saw him go into that diner on the corner across from the town hall. What was the name . . . Earl's?"

"You must be mistaken," Hallie said. "You must have seen someone else, someone who looked like him."

Newton shrugged. "Maybe so. But I thought you might enjoy reading one of his books. They're quite good. I've read them all. He really is a talented man."

"I'm sure he is," Hallie said softly.

Newton nodded, then slowly backed away from her. "Well, I'd better be going, now. I'll see you later, Hallie."

Hallie turned her gaze back to the sea. But a few moments later she found her eyes fixed on the photo of Tris that adorned the back of his book jacket. She stared at it, trying to plumb the depths of those pale blue eyes.

This was not the man she knew. He looked so remote, so emotionless. The man she knew was warm and caring and funny. The man she knew made her feel aware and alive. The man who looked up at her from the back of the book was not Tris.

Hallie closed her eyes. So was he two different men? She couldn't help but believe that she'd seen the real Tris behind the celebrity's face. When Tris was with her, he'd been himself, the man she'd fallen in love with.

But what about the other side of him, the side she didn't know? Would she have been able to love *that* man? She'd never really know, because Tris was gone and there would be no bringing him back.

Hallie slid off the rock and slowly walked back toward the inn, the book tucked beneath her arm. Her gaze scanned the facade of the inn and she smiled. She'd be all right. She had her home and the Sisters. Life was back to normal.

9

TRIS STOOD in the shadow of a shop doorway, watching the revelry on the main street of Egg Harbor. The
First Annual Egg Harbor Vampire Festival was well
under way and vampire lovers from around New England had invaded the quiet seacoast town. Townspeople manned booths selling everything from
"Vampire Burgers" to clusters of fresh garlic, and children scampered among the adult revelers, dressed in
their Halloween costumes.

This final night of the Vampire Festival coincided
with All Hallow's Eve and trick or treat, a perfect end-
ing to a perfectly bizarre public event. Tris glanced up
at the night sky. It was also the night of the new moon,
the night when Nicholas Tyler was said to appear on the
streets of Egg Harbor.

Tris was costumed like many others in a black cape
with a blood-red satin lining that he'd purchased from
the Ladies' League. He'd pulled the hood of the cape up
over his head to hide his identity even further, but most
of the crowd was either too crazy or too drunk to no-
tice him lurking in the shadows.

He found himself constantly scanning the crowd,
searching for a slender figure with dark hair and startling green eyes. He knew Hallie would never be a willing participant in a festival she'd fought so hard against.

But he hadn't seen her in almost a week and he couldn't help but long for a glimpse of her.

He'd found a place to stay down the coast from Egg Harbor, a nondescript room in a chain motel just off the interstate. Since he'd checked in, he hadn't written a word, which really didn't surprise him. He'd managed to convince himself that the only way he could work on his new novel was in the confines of the coach house with Hallie close by.

Damn, he missed her. He missed the time they spent together every night and he missed the soft, musical quality of her voice. Most of all, he missed the taste of her lips and the feel of her body beneath his hands. His mind flashed a memory of them together in the coach house, making love, and he bit back another curse.

He would make things right between them again. He'd spent the past five days working toward that very end. By day, he'd prowled the archives of the town newspaper and the Egg Harbor Historical Society, looking for any clue to the Tyler family vampire legend. By night, he watched the Tyler family graveyard, waiting patiently for the person who had deliberately planted the antique cuff link he'd found.

If he could only prove the legend a hoax, then perhaps Hallie might forgive him. Perhaps all the vampire mania would die down and the town would get back to normal. And after that, maybe the presence of Tristan Montgomery, bestselling novelist, might not cause such a stir.

Tris waited until the crowd had thinned, then stepped out of the doorway. Most of the activity for the festival centered on the main street of town. As he passed the town hall he noticed the banner announcing the dramatic production of Hallie's great-aunts, Prudence and Patience. The curtain would rise at precisely midnight for the staging of a scene from Alexandre Dumas's *The Vampire*, the final event of the day-long festival.

Tris glanced at his watch. Ten o'clock. He still hadn't paid his nightly visit to the Tyler family cemetery. If he hurried he could find out what was going on up there before coming back into town for the aunts' play. He tugged the hood of his cape further down on his head, then headed up the hill toward the Widow's Walk, keeping to the shadows all the way.

There had been no mention of the Tyler cemetery on the official program, nor had it been marked on the official map included in the program. No doubt, Hallie had refused to open the cemetery to festival visitors and had threatened the town council with all manner of retribution if they tried to capitalize on her uncle Nicholas. But plenty of visitors had tramped up to the Episcopal Cemetery searching for the grave and many of them were still gathered there when Tris arrived.

The church had had the good sense to lock the gate so people could only stare at the old grave markers from behind the tall iron fence. Tris joined the crowd for a short time, then silently slipped off into the woods. He quickly navigated the path with the aid of a small penlight, his cape fluttering out behind him.

When he arrived at the rusty iron gate, the cemetery was silent. He had expected Newton and his group from Undead International to be on watch as they had on previous nights, but they had probably found some other ghoulish activity to occupy their time.

Tris ran his hands along the bricks to the right of the gate, looking for the niche that hid the key to the gate. He found the loose brick, retrieved the key, and unlocked the gate, then put the key back in its hiding place.

A light mist had descended over the woods, growing thicker with every minute, making the feeble beam from his penlight useless. He stepped inside the tall brick walls and pulled the gate shut behind him. Dead leaves crackled beneath his feet and he stepped carefully, then stopped as he heard a loud rustling of footsteps outside the walls of the cemetery.

Silently, he slipped behind a tall monument and pulled his cape closer to his body. He watched as two figures fumbled with the brick until they found the key, then unlocked a gate that had already been unlocked. They stepped inside, making no effort to hide their presence, both holding large lanterns that illuminated nearly the entire graveyard.

"You be the lookout, Jonah," the first man said. "I'll plant the evidence."

"Hurry up, Silas!" Jonah replied. "If we get caught, this whole thing will blow up in our faces. I don't fancy bein' known as a swindler."

"Just hold yer water, Jonah. I got to make this look real."

Tris peered around the corner of the monument and watched as Silas Pemberton, mayor of Egg Harbor, stood over Nicholas Tyler's grave. The man poked around in the dirt a bit with his toe, then pulled a leather glove from his pocket and dropped it at his feet. "There, that should do it."

"Don't forget them finger holes," Jonah whispered from his place at the gate. "With all the trampling going on here, nobody's noticed them for a while."

Silas grunted, then bent and poked his fingers into the dirt at the base of the headstone.

"Make sure you put plenty of them in there," Jonah said. "It's supposed to show that the vampire's been trying to get out."

"Will you shut yer trap!" Silas snapped. "I know what I'm doin'!"

Satisfied that he'd completed his task to Jonah's exacting specifications, Silas straightened and lumbered toward the gate. "This is the end of it," he grumbled. "I don't ever wanna come back to this place again."

"At least not until next year's festival," Jonah said.

"Yeah, yeah, yeah. I don't know why I ever let you talk me into this. You know what would happen if we got caught? This whole town would turn on us. Folks in Egg Harbor pride themselves on their honesty and this is about as dishonest as it gets."

"What else are we supposed to do?" Jonah asked. "We got ourselves a vampire festival to run. We need to at least show that we might have a vampire or two in town."

"You really think these folks believe in vampires?" Silas asked.

Jonah shrugged. "Why else would they come?"

"Because most of them got a screw loose, you chowderhead! You talked to any of these yahoos? I tell ya, Jonah, some of them are downright spooky. They ain't got all their oars in the water."

"Spooky or not, they're spending money."

Silas grunted again. "They're not our real problem anyway. Hallie Tyler is. She's the one we've got to get to believe."

Jonah shook his head. "That's a tall order, Silas. Hallie Tyler's the most pig-headed woman in Egg Harbor. There's no changin' her mind once it's set. She's not dumb enough to fall for all this vampire stuff."

"But if we get her to believe, we've got ourselves a real draw for the festival. She's the key, Jonah. Right now, she's just a word away from calling this whole thing a sham. If that cravat didn't convince her, I don't know what will." Silas paused, then held up his hand. "You hear that?"

Jonah frowned. "Hear what?"

Silas hurried to the gate and peeked out. "Turn down that damn lantern! Come on, let's get out of here. Someone's coming."

Tris watched as the two men stumbled over each other to make it out of the cemetery without being seen. They quickly locked the gate behind them, then shoved the key back in its place and headed off through the woods, avoiding the path altogether.

A few moments later another pair appeared at the gate, lanterns held aloft. Tris smiled to himself as he recognized Prudence and Patience. He'd never expected the graveyard to be quite this busy tonight. But he'd already learned a lot more in five minutes than he had in five days of futile research.

"Shh! Step lightly, Sister. We must hurry. There are too many people about and we don't want to be seen."

"We shouldn't be here, Sister. The curtain rises on our play in less than two hours!"

Tris had never been able to tell the difference between the two sisters and tonight, from the shadows of the monument, he still couldn't. It didn't much matter which was Prudence and which was Patience, since they both seemed to be in a talkative mood.

"Don't be such a coward. If anyone catches us here, we'll just say we're visiting our dear uncle's grave...for creative inspiration. No one would suspect our real purpose."

"Must we do this?"

"We must. We are in far too deeply to go back now. Our future in Egg Harbor is at stake. If they learn the truth, we would become social pariahs, outcasts without a single person to call our friend."

They stepped into the cemetery, then both hurried over to Nicholas Tyler's grave. "But we were just little girls when this all began. Surely they would understand. Children make up stories. They mean no harm."

"I don't want to face the consequences if anyone learns that we fabricated the story about our uncle Nicholas. And neither do you!"

"No one will know! There is only one piece of proof and that is well hidden in the library at the inn. No one will ever find Mother's journal and no one will ever know that we are the ones who perpetrated this hoax."

"Just drop that cuff link and let's leave this place. I swear, I rue the day you made me read Mr. Stoker's novel."

He watched as one of the sisters carefully planted another clue at the base of the gravemarker, rearranging the leaves and dirt until she was well satisfied. She noticed neither the fresh finger holes nor the glove that Silas Pemberton had dropped a few minutes before.

One sister sighed dramatically. "I didn't make you read it, *you* made *me* read it. Don't you remember, Sister?"

"Oh, no. Your memory has failed you. It was the other way around, Sister."

"Well, it makes no difference now, Sister. We need a vampire and Uncle Nick is the closest thing we have to a member of the undead since Mr. Tristan decided to leave town."

They both looked at each other and sighed. "Poor Hallie," they said in tandem.

"She hasn't been the same since he left."

"I do believe she was in love with the man."

"It never pays to love a vampire. One can only be left with a broken heart. Or a nasty neck wound and eternal life."

With that said, the Sisters made their way to the gate and closed it behind them. Tris winced as he heard the lock click shut, knowing this time he'd have to scale the wall to get out. But just as he was about to hoist himself up onto a foothold in the wall, he heard the gate creak behind him again.

He jumped down and quickly found his hiding place, cursing beneath his breath. At this rate, he'd be lucky to get out of the graveyard by dawn. He peered around the monument and his breath caught in his throat as a slender figure made its way into the cemetery.

"Hallie," he murmured softly.

She hesitated, then turned and pointed her flashlight in his direction, but he remained well hidden and perfectly still. A moment later, the light skittered away and he leaned over and watched her.

She wore her jacket and her boots, but beneath, Tris could see her white nightgown fluttering in the wind. His mind drifted back to the night she had appeared at his door, dressed only in the nightgown and a shawl. He closed his eyes and tried to conjure an image of her naked beneath her gown. As the image became clearer, he felt himself grow hard with desire.

He wanted to step out from his hiding place and take her into his arms, to breathe in the scent of her and to kiss her like he'd dreamed of kissing her these last few days they'd spent apart. But instead, he pushed back his desire, knowing that the proper time would come soon.

Hallie did as all the others had and approached Nicholas Tyler's grave. Tris held his breath, waiting for her to drop another clue, yet all the while hoping she wouldn't. Hallie couldn't be part of the hoax, could she?

She bent and brushed at the leaves, searching the ground with her flashlight. He heard her gasp and a moment later, she picked up the glove Pemberton had left and carefully examined it beneath the light. Then she found the cuff link her aunts had dropped and seconds later, she stomped out the finger holes.

"Damn," she muttered to herself. "Who is doing this?" She glanced around the graveyard. "If I could only catch the person, this whole thing would go away."

She made a final search of the area, then stood and stared at her uncle's gravestone for a long time. Tris slowly stood, fighting the urge to go to her. He'd nearly decided to step out of his hiding place when she suddenly turned on her heel and rushed out the gate, leaving it open behind her.

Tris slipped out from behind the monument and stood in the gateway, watching Hallie disappear into the mist. "It won't be long now," he murmured to himself. "I'll make it right for you, Hallie. And then you'll have to admit your feelings for me. You won't be able to run away again."

THE INN WAS DARK when Tris arrived. He withdrew his key from his pocket and unlocked the front door, then quietly slipped inside. He'd been smart to keep the key after he'd checked out and lucky that Hallie had not asked for it back. As he closed the door behind him, the clock on the mantel chimed twice.

With soft footsteps, he headed for the small library just off the parlor, a room lined with bookshelves and dominated by an old oak library table. Light filtered in from the parlor providing enough illumination to search through the volumes, but he closed the door and flipped on the lamp anyway.

"All right, ladies," he murmured. "I know there's a journal in here somewhere. Now, where would you hide it?"

The journal would not be out in the open, for Patience and Prudence would never take the risk of Hallie seeing it. Putting it on the shelves with all the other books wouldn't be a wise choice, either. But where would they put it? Tris ruled out the higher shelves for the aunts were just barely five feet tall. Anything higher than six feet would be well out of their reach.

He closed his eyes and racked his brain for a clue. It would take him all night and most of the next day to search every shelf and pull out every book. His mind wandered back to the conversation he'd overheard in the graveyard.

"Bram Stoker," he murmured. He quickly scanned the shelves looking for the volume of Stoker's *Dracula*. A few minutes later he found it, in perfect alphabetical order by author and on a shelf low enough for the Sisters to reach. He pulled a stack of books off the shelf and searched behind them, but to his disappointment he found nothing but dust.

Tris cursed softly and stared at the partially cleared bookshelf. Reaching out, he tapped softly on the wall behind the shelf. The wall was made of tongue-and-groove wainscoting, varnished to a deep warm tone. As he reached the center of the shelf, a hollow thud sounded beneath his knuckles.

Tris rapped again, then peered more closely at the wall. A piece of the wainscoting was loose, loose enough to pry off with his fingers. Tris pulled the wood away and another piece came loose, revealing a small space within the wall of the library.

Tris smiled as he reached inside. His hand immediately came to rest on what felt like a book. Carefully, he withdrew the small volume and brought it into the light. He flipped through the yellowed pages, his eyes skimming across a spidery script. Could this be what he was looking for? Could this journal have belonged to the mother of Patience and Prudence?

If the book held a clue to the origins of the Tyler family vampire legend, he needed time to study it. Tris stepped to the door and listened for any sounds in the parlor. The inn remained silent and he decided to stay in the library until he found the clue he was looking for. He sat down at the library table and pulled the lamp closer.

The script was difficult to read with it's old-fashioned hand and faded pages. But Tris slowly got used to it and found himself fascinated by an account of the day-to-day life of a 1920s society matron. The daily accounts shifted as summer turned to winter, from the summer house in Egg Harbor to a home on Boston's Beacon Hill.

After an hour of reading Tristan finally found the passage he was looking for. He bent closer to the light and ran his finger along each line, studying the words carefully.

I am at my wit's end with Patience and Prudence. I fear their names were poorly chosen for neither is patient nor prudent. They have put their hands on a copy of Mr. Stoker's novel, Dracula, and started a rumor that my dear departed uncle Nicholas was a vampire. They are too young to be told the truth, yet I can't seem to stop them from perpetuating this story of theirs. How can I tell them that dear Nicholas drowned in the millpond after taking a drunken midnight swim with two of his disreputable ladyfriends? Nicholas never was much of a swimmer, nor could he hold his drink. I can only hope he at least found success with the ladies in his life before he passed on.

Tris slowly closed the journal and pressed it between his palms. He had the proof he needed. There was no Tyler family vampire. Old Uncle Nick's status as one of the undead was simply a fabrication by two very imaginative and irrepressible little girls.

He chuckled softly. He could just imagine Patience and Prudence making up such a wild tale. The Sisters seemed to thrive on small-town excitement and loved nothing better than to stir things up. It was no wonder they never married! Any man who married one, automatically got the other, and together they were way too much to deal with.

A smile touched his lips and he sighed in relief. The mystery was solved now and the sooner he talked to Hallie, the better. Tris pushed out of the chair and stood, then reached for the lamp and flipped it off. But as he slipped out of the darkened library, he froze at the sound of footsteps on the stairs.

Tris held to the shadows of the parlor and watched as a figure, dressed in pure white, paused at the foot of the stairs. She resembled a spirit, her nightgown translucent, her rumpled hair made luminous by the light in the stairwell behind her.

He held his breath and she took another step forward. She could sense his presence. He knew by the way her eyes darted around the room. His gaze skimmed along her body, her limbs visible through the thin fabric of her gown.

As if he could no longer keep himself from her, Tris stepped out of the shadows and into the spill of light from the stairwell. His gaze caught hers and she gasped softly, frozen by indecision.

Slowly, he approached, his satin cape rustling against his legs. He held out his hand and she stepped toward him, then pressed his palm against her warm cheek.

"You've come back," she said softly.

Tris shook his head. "I never left. I couldn't leave you, Hallie. We belong together."

"We do," she replied. "I know that now."

With a soft moan, he pulled her into his embrace and brought his mouth down on hers. He pressed her body against his, trying to mold every soft curve against him until he could feel her warmth seep through his clothes.

Slowly, they stumbled backward until Hallie came up against the wall. Tris pulled her leg up over his hip and leaned into her, his hard ridge branding the soft skin of her belly. He wanted to make love to her right there in the parlor; he wanted to strip the gown from her body and gaze at her nakedness until he could wait no longer.

He slid his palms along her hips, bunching the fabric in his fists until his fingers met soft skin. "You feel so good, sweetheart," he murmured against her neck.

Her hand came down between them and she gently rubbed his shaft through the fabric of his jeans. She moved to work at the top button and Tris closed his eyes, trying to control his need for release but anticipating the feel of her hand on him. He took a ragged breath and nuzzled her neck.

Suddenly, stars exploded in his head. He felt himself falling, his legs crumpling beneath him and then everything went black.

"Tris?" Hallie said softly.

She struggled to hold his limp body upright, but she

was quickly losing her grip. "Tris, are you all right?" His knees buckled and he slid down the length of her, falling to a heap at her feet.

Hallie bent down, her heart pounding with fear, and gave him a shake. "Tris? Tris, wake up. I'm sorry, I didn't mean to—"

"Do you think he's dead?"

Startled, Hallie looked up to find Prudence and Patience standing above her. Prudence held a small garden spade in her hand and Patience clutched a wooden stake in front of her.

"He can't be dead," Prudence said. "You're still holding the stake. Turn him over, Hallie, so we can drive it into his wicked heart."

Hallie stared at them in astonishment. "What have you two done?" She gazed at the garden spade. "Did you hit him with that?"

Prudence nodded. "We were trying to protect you, Hallie. He was about to bite your neck. Now step back so we can finish the job."

"You'll do no such thing!" Hallie carefully rolled Tris over onto his back and peered down at his pale face. "Did you hit him on the head?"

"That's what I was aiming for," Prudence said. "But I'm afraid I wasn't able to hit him very hard. I just grazed him." She grasped the handle of the spade and swung it like a baseball bat. "I've never been good with shovels. We always had a gardener to take care of these things."

"To take care of what?" Hallie demanded. "Assaulting guests in this house with garden tools?"

Patience sighed. "But, dear, he's not a guest. He's a vampire."

Hallie scrambled to her feet, cursing vividly as she flipped on the lights in the parlor. She quickly returned to Tris's side and patted him gently on the cheek. He moaned softly and turned his head. She carefully examined him for any blood, but found only a small knot on the crown of his head.

Patience bent down beside her and stared into Tris's face. "Can't you see, Hallie? He's wearing a cape just like Dracula."

"So are half the people in this town," Hallie muttered. "It's a costume."

"Now let's see his teeth." Patience reached out to push his lip up, but Hallie slapped her hand.

Tris's eyes fluttered open and Patience scrambled to her feet, retreating a safe distance to Prudence's side. Tris frowned as he gazed up at Hallie. "Wh-what happened?" He tried to sit up, but then flopped back down on the floor and rubbed the back of his head. "Jeez, what hit me?"

"My aunt Prudence and a small shovel," Hallie said.

"Your aunt Prudence and a—" He groaned and covered his eyes. "And is she carrying a wooden stake, as well?"

"No," Hallie said. "But Patience is."

This time Tris was able to push himself to a sitting position. He frowned up at the aunts and slowly shook his head. "I should have known," he said.

Hallie took his arm and helped him to the sofa, then sat next to him, watching him in concern. "Are you all right? Maybe we should call a doctor," she said.

"I'm fine," Tris muttered.

"You should have hit him harder, Sister," Patience murmured.

Hallie shot to her feet and grabbed the garden spade from Prudence's hands. Then she snatched the wooden stake from Patience and stalked to the front door. "We will not be needing these tonight," she said as she tossed them outside.

The aunts watched Hallie and Tris from a safe distance across the parlor. Hallie brushed Tris's hair back from his temples and looked into his eyes. "You're sure you're all right?"

He gave the aunts a sideways glance. "They think I'm a vampire, don't they?" he whispered.

Hallie nodded and pressed her forehead against his. "That's where I got the idea," she murmured. "When they get a notion into their heads, it's impossible to knock it loose."

"Like the story about your uncle Nicholas?" Tris asked.

Hallie shrugged. "I'm not sure where that story started, but they've certainly done their share to keep it alive."

Tris straightened, then reached out and took Hallie's hands into his. "I know where the story started," he said. "And I think it's about time you did, too."

Hallie watched as Tris slowly got to his feet and walked toward the aunts. "Ladies, I think you'd better sit down. We have a lot to talk about."

The aunts stared up at him with wide eyes, but then quickly scurried to do as they were told. They took a place on the love seat and stared up at Tris warily, watching his every move, as if he might bite them.

"If you think you have any power over us, you're wrong," Prudence said. "My sister and I are immune to the powers of the undead."

"Well, you won't be needing those powers tonight," Tris explained. "Because I'm not undead. Never have been. And the only power I have tonight is the power to reveal the truth. Don't you think it's time for the truth, ladies?"

Hallie found herself amazed at his patient yet firm tone. After all, the Sisters had just tried to knock him silly with a shovel, and they were both bent on murder with a wooden stake. They still persisted in the belief that he was a vampire. Yet Tris hadn't even come close to losing his temper with them.

The Sisters glanced at each other, then back at Tristan. "What truth would that be?" Patience asked.

"Why don't we start with a short reading?" Tris reached inside his cape and withdrew an old book. "I found this in the library. I think it's appropriate to the occasion."

Patience and Prudence gasped in surprise and frantically began to whisper to each other, leaving Hallie to wonder what Tris might possibly read that could upset them so.

"I believe I'll start with this entry written by your mother in her personal journal," he said. Slowly he read the words that proved where the legend of Nicholas Tyler had started while Hallie listened in astonishment. When he finished, he slapped the book shut and handed it to her.

Hallie stared down at it, then stood and moved to his side. "You started this whole thing?" she demanded, her gaze resting on the aunts.

Tris patted her on the hand. "I don't think we're quite finished, sweetheart. Why don't you sit down. There's much more. I'd suggest we move on to the graveyard now," Tris said. "And all the clues that appeared at Uncle Nicholas's grave."

"You know about the clues?" Hallie asked as she took her place on the sofa.

Tris nodded. "And I'm not the only one."

Hallie frowned. "Newton found a silk cravat there. And I found a signet ring. And a kid glove and a cuff link. And you were there when we found the scrimshaw button and the finger holes."

"The cuff link you found matches one I found," Tris said. "And I believe both were placed there by your aunts."

Hallie glared at them again, unable to believe the complexity of their lies. "Is that true? *You* were putting clues in the graveyard?"

"We thought it was the only way," Prudence said. "The story had gotten well out of hand and we just didn't know what to do."

"What about the scrimshaw button?"

"We tore it from one of Uncle Nick's shirts that we found in the attic. We put the signet ring there, as well. But we know nothing about the cravat or the glove. Those must have been left by Uncle Nick. That's the only explanation."

"I believe those came from Silas Pemberton," Tris said.

Hallie gasped. "You got the mayor involved in your scheme?"

Patience shook her head. "Oh, no! We've told no one. I swear!"

"It's true," Prudence added. "We were afraid if it became known, that no one would associate with us anymore. We had no choice. Everyone had come to depend on the existence of our family vampire. We were just trying to make everyone happy."

Tris sat down on the sofa and wove his fingers through Hallie's. "I think the mayor and the rest of the town council did this on their own, Hallie. I saw Silas Pemberton plant the glove and I suspect the cravat was from him as well."

"But it's monogrammed with Uncle Nick's initials. How could he have gotten it out of our attic?"

"I'd venture to guess that the cravat is old but the monogramming is new. He probably bought that and the glove in some antique store along the coast. The mayor and the town council were willing to do just about anything to perpetuate the hoax your aunts started. I think a little talk with him about the facts of the situation might make him see your point on the tourism issue."

"You're going to tell him?" Patience asked in a worried tone.

Hallie raised a brow, then shook her head. "No, *we* are. First thing tomorrow morning, before Silas and his cronies have a chance to make any plans for next year's festival, we're all going down to pay our upstanding mayor a little visit."

"But—"

Hallie held up her hand to stop their response. "No excuses. You're going." She sighed, then glanced up at the clock on the mantel. "Now you'd both better get to bed. We've got a busy day in front of us tomorrow. Besides our visit with the mayor, you still have to haul all those pumpkins out of your room. I don't think they'll be turning into vampires anytime soon."

Patience and Prudence rose from the love seat and shuffled past Hallie and Tris, their expressions tinged with utter dejection.

"One other thing," Hallie said, stopping their exit. "If you knew the story about Uncle Nick was a hoax, how could you believe Tris was a vampire? Did you really believe in vampires or was that just part of the scheme?"

"We could only hope," Patience said with a dramatic sigh.

"It was the only way out of the mess we'd made," Prudence finished.

Hallie watched as her two great-aunts climbed the stairs to their room. Then she smiled and looked back at Tris. "I'm sorry for all the trouble they caused you."

"Caused us," Tris said, pulling her closer.

Hallie snuggled against him and rested her head on Tris's shoulder as she stared into the dark depths of the fireplace. "I guess it's all over," she said.

Tris caught her chin between his thumb and forefinger and turned her gaze to his. "It's far from over Hallie. You and I still have a lot to talk about. Now that the town's vampire problem is solved, we're going to need to solve the problem of our impending wedding."

Hallie's eyes widened and she pulled back. "Our wedding?"

"Yes, our wedding," Tris said, brushing his mouth against hers. "I've been alone for so long, Hallie. I didn't think I needed anyone until I met you. And now I can't imagine living without you." He cupped her cheek in his palm. "I intend to marry you, Hallie Tyler. And unless you agree right now, I'm sure we're going to have more problems in store for us over the next few months."

Hallie smiled. "Like what?" she demanded.

"Like finishing the renovations on the coach house, like selling my apartment in New York, like how many children we're going to have and—"

"Children?" she asked.

Tris stared deeply into her eyes. He paused for a long moment before he spoke. "I had two parents, but never really felt as if we were a family," he said, a trace of resignation in his voice. "I want to make a home with you, Hallie. A big, happy home full of love and children. Lots and lots of children."

Hallie placed her finger over his lips and stared up into his gaze. "I think we can discuss the numbers later," she said. "Now, why don't you ask me again, Tris."

"Ask you what?" he teased, mumbling the words from behind her finger.

"You *know* what."

He pulled her hand away and held it in his, then stared into her eyes until she was certain he could see every ounce of love in her soul. "Will you marry me, Hallie? Will you give me the family I never had? Will you make my life perfect?"

A tear sprang to the corner of Hallie's eye and she brushed it away. "I will marry you, Edward Tristan Montgomery. We'll make wonderful children together. And I will love you forever."

Tris pulled Hallie into his arms and kissed her then, a kiss filled with promise for a lifetime together. And at that moment, Hallie knew that he would never leave her and that their love would be nothing less than immortal.

Epilogue

HALLIE SAT at her dressing table and brushed her hair, staring at herself distractedly in the mirror. A cool draft fluttered the lace curtains of the bedroom and she shivered, rubbing her bare arms and sighing. The thin strap from her white lace nightgown slipped down over her shoulder and she slowly tugged it up, then reached for her perfume bottle.

Lazily, she pulled the stopper and dragged it along her collarbone, smiling at herself in the mirror. The curtain fluttered again and a dark form emerged from the shadows near the window. He was dressed in a black cape with a blood-red lining.

She watched him approach in the mirror, a smile curling the corners of her mouth. "I knew you'd come," she said.

"I heard you calling out to me," he said softly, his fingers toying with the strap of her nightgown. Gently, he pushed it down over her shoulder, then brushed her shoulder with his lips.

"Are they all gone?" she asked. She tipped her head to the side as his mouth moved to her neck.

"Mmm," he said. "We're all alone."

"You never were able to stay away from me for long," Hallie said.

Tris chuckled, his breath soft against her ear. "I thought it was the other way around," he murmured. He reached down and placed his hand over her swollen stomach. "How's my little vampire doing tonight?"

"He's kicking up a storm. Did we have enough candy for all the trick-or-treaters?"

Tris nodded. "Plenty. I gave them all double. One piece for coming up the path to the coach house in the dark and another for screaming after I gave them a good scare."

"Tris! They're just kids."

Tris slowly slid the other strap of her nightgown over her shoulder. "I do have a reputation to uphold, Mrs. Montgomery. I wouldn't want to disappoint the people of Egg Harbor. After all, half of them once thought I was a vampire."

"I never thought you were a vampire."

His eyebrow shot up and he turned her around on her chair until she faced him. He looked down at her and smiled. "Never?"

"Well, my common sense told me you weren't a vampire. But I knew you were just a little wicked."

He knelt down in front of her and pulled her knees along either side of his torso. "And you couldn't resist my wicked ways, could you?"

Hallie wrapped her arms around his neck, "I've never been able to resist you, Tristan Montgomery."

He placed his ear against her tummy and sighed. "Do you know how happy you make me, Hallie?"

Hallie ran her fingers gently through his hair. "How happy?"

"I never thought family was important. From the time I was a kid, I convinced myself that I was better off alone. And now I can't imagine living without you. Or our baby."

"I can't imagine living without you, either, Tris."

"Prove it," he said.

Hallie wriggled in his arms. "Take me to bed and I will."

With that, Tris stood and scooped her up, then carried her to the bed. He gently lowered her to the mattress and laid down beside her, placing his head on her stomach.

Hallie ran her fingers through her husband's hair and smiled to herself. After almost a year of marriage, she wondered if she'd ever tire of her husband's wicked ways. She closed her eyes and pulled him closer.

Not anytime soon, she said to herself as he reached out and ran his finger seductively down her arm. Not anytime soon.

This month's
irresistible novels from

Temptation

AN INCONVENIENT PASSION by Debra Carroll

Joanna Clooney was forced to ask her ex-husband, Reid, to
pretend they were still married to help her mother to recover
from a life-threatening illness. But their marriage of convenience
turned into an impossible sexually-charged charade as they
fought their attraction. There was only one place it could end—
in bed!

CALL ME by Alison Kent

It wasn't Harley Golden's style to call a perfect stranger and
have phone sex. But after one brief encounter with the
unforgettable Gardner Barnes, she was doing all sorts of
impulsive, adventurous things—like flying to see him, falling in
love, getting pregnant...

WICKED WAYS by Kate Hoffmann

Innkeeper Hallie Tyler's life is in chaos. The inn is filled to
capacity, thanks to her two imaginative aunts' decision to
resurrect—and embellish—an old family legend. Now she's
overrun with vampire chasers. But what's worse, Hallie finds
herself falling for the sexy, enigmatic Tristan Montgomery...who
seems to show an unusual interest in her neck...

THE OUTLAW by JoAnn Ross

Rogues

Wolfe Longwalker is about to be lynched for a crime he didn't
commit. Until Noel Giraudeau, a modern-day princess, finds
herself in 1896 Arizona, rescuing him. On the run from the law,
their passionate adventure quickly turns into something much
more real...but Noel's destiny is back in her own time.

Spoil yourself next month
with these four novels from

Temptation®

MIDNIGHT TRAIN FROM GEORGIA by Glenda Sanders

The Wrong Bed

When Erica O'Leary hears that her grandmother needs her, she
jumps on a train bound for Baltimore. Tired and eager to escape
a group of rowdy lawyers, she's glad she'd reserved a sleeper.
But Eric Sean O'Leary gets the surprise of his life when he finds
the beautiful, half-naked Erica sleeping in *his* bed!

HOLDING OUT FOR A HERO by Vicki Lewis Thompson

Mail Order Men

He was six feet tall and drop-dead gorgeous; Tanner Jones's
advertisement was answered immediately by Dori Mae Fitzpatrick.
But when they eventually meet, he discovers that she'd 'forgotten'
to mention either her young son or her obnoxious ex-husband. But
he, too, hadn't been entirely open—he was actually filthy rich—
something that Dori just couldn't abide...

A WISH FOR LOVE by Gina Wilkins

Bailey Gates had had enough of picking guys loaded down with
emotional baggage but one look at the enigmatic, sexy Ian Cameron
and she was smitten. However, Ian has a problem that even Bailey
isn't ready to take on. Because seventy five years ago Ian Cameron
was shot dead in cold blood...

ALL SHOOK UP by Carrie Alexander

Kate Mallory's caught four wedding bouquets in two years, but no
man. She decides to take matters into her own hands—in her own
logical way! But when she meets lusty bartender Jamie Flynn life
gets totally shaken up, as Jamie vows to take the pragmatic Kate
from a passionless spritzer to a wild margarita!

MILLS & BOON®

To HAVE & TO HOLD

Celebrate the joy, excitement and sometimes
mishaps that occur when planning that special
wedding in our treasured four-story collection.

Written by four talented authors—
Barbara Bretton, Rita Clay Estrada,
Sandra James and Debbie Macomber

Don't miss this wonderful short story collection
for incurable romantics everywhere!

Available: April 1997   Price: £4.99

Penny Jordan

New York Times bestselling author of
Power Play and *Cruel legacy*

POWER GAMES

The arrival of a mysterious woman threatens
a son's manipulative hold over his
millionaire father in PENNY JORDAN'S
latest blockbuster—a supercharged tale of
family rivalries

AVAILABLE IN PAPERBACK
FROM MARCH 1997

SANDRA BROWN

New York Times bestselling author

HONOUR BOUND

Theirs was an impossible love

"One of fiction's brightest stars!"
—Dallas Morning News

**Lucas Greywolf was Aislinn's forbidden
fantasy—and every moment of their
mad dash across Arizona drew her
closer to this unyielding man.**